THE
CRASH

JENN LEES

COMMUNITY CHRONICLES BOOK 1: A NOVELLA

Preface

Thank you for purchasing *The Crash*.

This prequel novella is an introduction to the world in which I set the *Community Chronicles Series* (a fictitious Scottish future) and doesn't involve time travel. The primary story begins with Caitlin and Scott in *Stolen Time: Community Chronicles Book 2* (which is the first novel I wrote in this series) and is a *different kind of time travel romance*.

I trust you will enjoy this introduction and read on.

If you join my newsletter group, you will receive a free eBook.

Join at www.jennleeswriter.com

Contents

Chapter One

Martin Moffatt darted a glance sideways at his cousin, Caitlin, as she snapped shut the reloaded firearm. Damn, she was fast. Martin slotted two cartridges down the side-by-side and placed it in the out-stretched hand of the lady guest in front of him. These shoots his father held at their Scottish Lowland country estate were usually a breeze, but this weekend Caitlin had made it a nightmare. She was *so* competitive.

"Who's winning?" Martin's father threw him a smile before shouting, "Pull!"

A volley of gunfire echoed across the heather-covered moor at the top of their property. The pheasant weren't co-operating today, so Martin and Caitlin had set up the clay-trap beside a clump of bracken fern where the machine flew the clay-pigeons out and up. They had to keep the guests happy.

"I am, of course, Uncle Kieran." Caitlin spared Martin a glance. With one hand she grabbed the used shotgun from the grasp of the gentleman guest in front of her, and with the other, thrust a reloaded small-bore sporting rifle into his waiting hand. She snapped open the shotgun she held. Two spent cartridges flicked out in no time.

Martin took the shotgun from the lady guest in front of him and handed her a newly loaded firearm. The woman's eyes narrowed as she took it.

Caitlin had tied her long blonde hair back like she wore it at work. Martin had dropped in there to see her once.

Bad move.

It had been a chaotic day in the Edinburgh Royal Infirmary Emergency Department where Caitlin was a nurse. She had asked him to never come to her workplace again. Martin hadn't ever visited her at her flat, either.

Martin managed a disgruntled huff as he stood behind the lady guest. He and Caitlin lived in the same city during the week, but they never crossed paths. Maybe she'd go to Majorca with the family this year. One could live in hope.

"Daydreaming won't get my gun reloaded, sonny." The narrowed eyes of the woman in front of him stared into his face.

"Oh, okay." Martin snapped shut the firearm he'd filled with two cartridges and handed it to the lady guest, then grabbed the shotgun she held under his nose.

Man, he had to concentrate. No wonder Caitlin was winning their bet. She was always so focused.

"Pull!" His father's authoritative voice bellowed out and another round of gunfire ensued.

Martin fumbled with the cartridges as he shoved them into the over-under shotgun.

"Fat-finger syndrome today, cuz?" Caitlin's blue eyes flicked up from one more reloaded firearm.

"Leave me alone, bully," Martin teased.

"A few free coffees from that place you work at on the Mile will do, Mista Barista."

"Okay," Martin sighed. "You've won."

"Where's my gun?" The lady guest spun around to face him; a vertical line creased her brow above her nose and her eyes narrowed to slits. "Less talk. More reloading."

With the shoot finished, Martin's father drove the guests back to the main house, while Martin and Caitlin collected the firearms, ammunition, trap, and left-over clays, and loaded them into the SUV. Martin drove the vehicle down the moor's narrow track. They called it the Lowlands, but this part of Scotland had undulating hills carpeted in greens and dark browns. Today, clouds dragged themselves over the hills whose sides would soon be an eruption of purple as the summer brought the heather into bloom. Warmth burst in Martin's chest. He'd spent his life, from early teens until recently, living on this estate after his father had built his electronics business and made his fortune. Martin had had some great times with his father then, who had been able to relax and spend time with his children after years away building his business.

"You're very quiet." Caitlin broke into his reverie. "But then, you're never one for small talk. Or are you just mad at me for beating you?"

"No." Martin laughed as he shook his head. "Couldn't be mad at you."

"Mr Silent Man, that's what you are."

"Am I?" He threw his half-smile at her.

"So, what *are* you?" She pressed.

"Physics student."

"You like that, don't you? Makes people think you're intelligent." Caitlin squinted. "And?"

"Son of a wealthy man."

"So, you see yourself as that." She didn't hold back her critical tone. "A rich kid?"

"Well, I am." He shrugged. "Dad worked hard for it. Why not?"

"You're more than that." Caitlin smiled and turned to look out the window.

They drove through a small wood of silver birch and ash as the main house, a double story Georgian mansion, came into view. Barley fields lay either side of the house. A sample of the next batch of scotch made by the local distillery, using their barley, would arrive soon. He dropped Caitlin off at the back door, and then parked the vehicle in one of the garages that sat in a row behind the house.

As Martin made his way to the front door, the late afternoon sun angled beams of gold through the doorway and large windows, illuminating the paintings hanging on the walls of the front vestibule. Scenes of Scottish lochs hung beside portraits of past lairds. A fan of Lochaber axes glinted next to a display of claymores mounted on the bare-stone wall.

Caitlin stepped out of the front door with her bags in her hands and walked to her car parked in one of the parking spaces at the front of the house.

"Leaving already?" Martin followed and leaned against his luxury class sedan parked next to her two-door run-about.

"Yes. Some of us have to work. I'm not a uni student anymore."

"Dig. Dig." He crossed his arms over his chest. "I do work, you know. Here and at *The Mile of Coffee*."

"You owe me some of its wares. I like cappu—"

"—ccino. I know. And you'll get it. Just come in and claim your prize when I'm working. Darren, my boss, doesn't give away freebies."

Caitlin smiled and threw her bag into the back seat. Her blonde hair had come loose from its tie and brushed the pale skin of her neck.

"Are you coming to Dad's birthday party?" Martin asked.

"Of course." She sat in the driver's seat and turned the ignition key. Nothing happened.

"Going already, Caitlin?" Theresa's voice came from behind him, grating his nerves as usual.

"It appears not." Martin turned to his older sister. Theresa had a way of belittling Caitlin and she did it every time. Like it was her hobby. "Try it again, Caitlin."

Caitlin's hand turned the key as her mouth screwed to one side.
Nothing.

"You need a mechanic." Theresa was on to it—as usual. "There's one in town. Not the wee village, the town. Phone him up, he'll be here in no time."

"The call-out fee will be more than I can afford." Caitlin's shoulders slumped.

Theresa tilted her head and pursed her lips.
Like she even cares.

"Pull the bonnet. I'll have a look." Martin moved to the front of the car.

"What do you know about cars, Martin?" Theresa asked. "Does theoretical physics cover the internal combustion engine?"
Yeah, Theresa denigrate my studies once more.

"I do know a wee bit about cars," he snapped.

Lifting the bonnet, Martin pushed his hair out of his eyes and tucked it behind his ear. He examined the engine while he clicked the fingers of his left hand. Then he twiddled some wires and tubing. It was an easy fix. "Try it now."

Caitlin tried the ignition key. This time the engine turned, stuttered, and went quiet.

"And again," Martin called.

He looked through the windscreen. Caitlin's face flooded with relief as the engine came to life and stayed there. A smile tugged at the corners of Martin's mouth and he shut the bonnet while Caitlin revved the engine.

"Thanks, Martin. You've saved me." Caitlin's face lit up with her smile. "But you still owe me a coffee!" Her index finger pointed his way.

"Okay. See ya next week."

Chapter Two

S hona McGrath's feet burned with tiredness, but that was usual after a waitressing shift. The afternoon rush at the restaurant had tapered off early and her train from the centre of Edinburgh hadn't been the usual peak hour crush.

Thankfully.

She trudged up the street to her family home, a terraced house in a row of six along the street in the outer Edinburgh suburb of Wester Hailes. Dogs barked as children played on the swings in the playground nearby. The rain-soaked, over-grown hedge wet her shoulder as she brushed past walking through her gate and up the path to the front door.

A smoke haze filled the hallway, and she walked through it with the theme music of her mum's favourite television drama blaring from the living room.

"Hi, Mum." Shona peered into the dark room lit by flickering images from the television, which was on twenty-four-seven.

"Oh, hello darlin'. Ye hame early?" Her mother paused mid-drag on her cigarette. "What's wrong?"

"The afternoon slowed. The crash and all."

"What crash?" Her mother leaned forward on the sofa, her belly jiggling with her effort. "Anyone hurt?"

"No, Mam, the stock market crash. Have ye no' been watchin' the news, like?" Shona stood at the doorway, pushing off her work shoes from the heel with her toes. "It looks bad."

Her mother returned a blank stare.

"'Cos I've finished early, I'm plannin' to go to the protest later, aye?"

Her mother crossed her arm over her ample belly and placed the cigarette in her mouth, taking another long pull. She blew out after a moment. Two plumes of smoke flew out, one from each nostril. Shona stopped herself from making the fire-breathing-dragon comment her wee brother loved to say.

"Ye'll still get me ma supper, aye?" Her mother asked.

"Aye, Mum." Shona walked to the kitchenette and dumped her bag on the table amongst the junk mail and post.

On the fridge door, a large blue fridge magnet with 'Yes' in bold white letters held an overdue Scottish Power bill in place. A dark-blue magnet encircled by yellow stars stating 'bugger brexit', sat next to it. Shona opened the freezer section.

"Pizza or pasta, Mum?" she yelled into the living room.

"Pizza."

Shona left the kitchen with the microwave heating dinner and walked across the hall to her bedroom. The saltire hanging in her front window gave the room a bluish hue. Shona stripped out of her uniform and changed into jeans and jumper. She lifted her denim jacket from her chair and picked up a badge from her dresser. She pinned the Scottish flag next to her Equality badge, brushed her hair and touched up her lipstick. The microwave pinged in the kitchenette.

"You goin' tae eat something, Shona darlin'?" Mum asked as Shona handed her the pizza on a plate.

"No, I think I'll go back to Edinburgh and grab something on ma way to this protest outside parliament." Shona stepped to the kitchenette and grabbed her bag from among the clutter on the small table. She cleared it often, but it always returned to its usual state.

"What's this about, now? This protest?"

"Mum, the stock market has crashed again."

"Aye, well, that does nae bother me. I've nae money."

"It could, Mum. Banks are closing. The Government's got tae do somethin' about it, like."

Her mother raised her eyebrows. "Oh, aye. Good luck wi' that, lass."

"Well, if we all just sit in front of the TV, they'll no do nothin' for sure."

Her mother's hand stopped on its way to her mouth. The pizza she held dropped its cheese and tomato topping back onto the plate. Shona's face heated at the pained expression on her mum's face.

"Sorry, Mum. I ken you'd work if ye could."

The omnibus edition of Mum's favourite soapie continued to fill the room with its dramas. Her mum took a bite of the topping-less pizza. Shona shuffled her feet.

"Can I get you anything?"

"No." Mum took another bite.

Shona turned to go. "Goodbye, then."

"Ye wud nae have any cash on ye, like, darlin'?"

Shona's shoulders slumped. It was her payday, and her mum knew it.

"Aye. How much do ye need?"

"Och, a tenna wud do." Her mother's face brightened. "Your faither will be hame soon and he'll be needing some things at the wee shop, like."

Aye, the shop next to the betting agency.

Shona handed her mum the ten-pound note, pecked her on the cheek, and strode out the door, sighing heavily as it closed behind her.

Chapter Three

In *The Mile of Coffee*, a café on the Royal Mile in Edinburgh, the television on the wall was usually silent with subtitles. Today, Darren, Martin's boss, had switched it to a higher volume while the patrons listened. Martin caught snippets of the news in between orders of flat whites, lattés, and cappuccinos. At first, customers sat in partial disinterest at the activity of the stock market. It had fallen three days ago, and the slide continued. Now, by late afternoon, every person in the café watched intently as scenes of unrest in London filled the screen. The section of London where the world's banks headquarters were situated, was awash with a boisterous crowd. Riot police were gathering. News from other major cities broadcast glass-smashed store fronts and looters running off with televisions and other goods.

"What's going on?" Davy, a young guy who worked as a waiter, frowned up at the screen. "Why are people going crazy?"

"People were hit hard last time," Darren answered. "It's fallen quicker than 2008. And still going. People are afraid they'll lose their pension funds and savings."

"People are a bit panicky. I had to step out onto the road to get past a crowd at an ATM on my way to work this morning." Martin made another skinny latté at the espresso machine for the cute girl in the booth near the front window. "Most of them didn't get anything cos it was already empty."

"What was?" Davy's wide eyes darted back to Martin; hands poised in the middle of stacking clean dishes.

"The ATM."

"Most of the smaller banks have closed." Darren turned back to the news reports. "And two of the Big Five. Two of my pals' banks have requested they pay up a fair percentage of what's owed on their business mortgages. Banks are nervous. People just need to calm down. If they panic, it'll be a disaster." Darren took a deep breath.

"You're okay, aren't you Darren?" Davy turned his frown to their boss, looking like an alarmed hedgehog with his short-cropped hair stuck up with gel.

Darren cocked his head. "Aye. So far."

Martin closed the door of *The Mile of Coffee* after finishing his shift, zipping up his jacket and lighting a cigarette. At least with his father's wealth, this sudden drop in the market wouldn't affect him. Further up the Royal Mile, Edinburgh Castle sat rain-washed. He turned and headed down the Mile, walking past shop fronts of buildings that were centuries old. Rain made the sandstone a dirty-yellow and the greystone even greyer. He passed entrances to wynds and vennels. Breezes funnelled through them, blowing his exhaled cigarette smoke into his long fringe. The malty smell of beer wafted out as he walked by taverns. Bagpipe music and jaunty Scottish Ceilidh tunes blared out of the souvenir shops. Tours advertised on placards promised history and ghosts, while snippets of English in various accents, Asian languages, and an abundance of European tongues, surrounded him.

Ahead, at the far end of the Royal Mile near Holyrood, a crowd gathered, spilling onto the street at the side of the Scottish Parliament building, the modern deal that looked so out of place opposite the seventeenth-century architecture of Holyrood Palace. The angry voices of the crowd rose up along The Mile.

Martin hunched into his jacket; his designer trousers were wet at the cuffs already. He needed some cash, so he headed left down North Bridge to Princes Street.

He'd been a fool about Caitlin. At his father's birthday party, Martin had caught part of a conversation between Caitlin and Great Aunt Meredith. Caitlin had said when she met the right man, Aunt Meredith would be the first to know. So, if *he* was the right man, she'd met him already, right?

Wrong.

Man, that was *so* creepy. What was he thinking? Caitlin was his first cousin, for heaven's sake!

Martin mentally shook himself.

The rumbling of trains continued underneath him as he walked the bridge over Waverly Station. The smash and clatter of glass breaking echoed toward him, its sharpness snapping him out of his self-reproach. Ahead, a mob clambered into broken shop windows and emerged with armfuls of goods.

Martin stopped in his tracks. He could get to an ATM nearer his flat in Newington. Stubbing his cigarette butt under his shoe, he turned and made his way to the bus stop. His phone vibrated crazily in his jacket pocket. He took it out and glanced at the screen. It was his father.

"Yeah?"

"Don't go to the estate." Instead of its usual cheeriness, his father's voice was haggard.

"Wasn't planning to. What's up?"

"We were attacked. The place ransacked—"

"Wait. Slow down, Dad!"

"Caitlin's missing. They took her—"

"Who did? What happened?" Thudding began in Martin's chest.

"Bloody rent-a-mob! Hooligans riding on the back of this trouble and looking for fun came and trashed the place. I got your mother out. I couldn't..." His voice broke.

"Dad?" Martin's heart rocked his ribcage.

Ragged breathing came through the phone. "When they'd gone, I went back. I left your mother in the summer house by the loch. I couldn't find her. Her horse was gone."

"Who? Caitlin?"

"Aye. She's staying with us for the summer, remember? She may have got on Bonnie, her mare, and got away but..."

"But what?" The thumping now hit his temples.

"There's no sign of her or the guy we hired for the summer...and Andy's dead."

"What?" Ice hit his chest now. Poor Andy the groundsman wasn't a young man. And those bastards had got him. What would they do to Caitlin?

"I'm coming down, Dad."

"No! Don't! It's not safe. We're not there."

"What did the police say?"

"They told us not to go back and they'll look for Caitlin. But...they're overloaded. Have you seen what's going on?"

Behind Martin, the noise of the approaching crowd grew louder.

"Dad, I've got to go. I'll phone you when I get to my flat. I can't believe they took Caitlin. We've got to find her."

"We will, son. Keep safe."

Martin turned and strode up the incline to the Royal Mile and crossed to his bus stop. His mind spun with possible plans. He'd ignore his dad and drive down anyway. Or catch the train.

He must get to his parents.

Chapter Four

Every petrol station Martin drove past had a queue. At least the queue to the one he now approached wasn't halfway down the street. A couple of cars pulled away, so he joined the line, rolling his German make car forward each time a vehicle left the queue. Before he reached the bowser, the service station attendant came out and attached a sign scratched on a piece of torn cardboard to the entry post.

Out of Fuel.

What! Another one? If only he'd fuelled up after coming back from the estate after his father's birthday. He'd burned down the motorway and almost burned up the last of his petrol. The fuel gauge was on empty and he'd be pushing his car to his flat if he didn't get some fuel soon. Panic buying had left everyone short. Martin crawled his car back to his flat and parked it.

He ran upstairs and slammed the door behind him before opening his small fridge. A can of beer lay next to some mouldy pâté and out-of-date Parma ham. Two cans of baked beans and an unopened packet of dry pasta were all that sat in his cupboard. The day couldn't get worse, surely?

Staring at his bare shelves, he pulled out his mobile and dialled his father's number.

"Hi Dad. How's Mum?"

"She's fine, Martin. Just a little shocked."

"Have they found Caitlin?"

"No, son, but they're searching for her."

"There isn't any petrol in the city. Panic buying." He fought to control the uneasiness and a panic of his own swirling in his mind. "I'll catch the train. Where are you now?"

"No, don't come down, Martin. We're okay. You stay there, and we'll let you know what's going on."

"But I—"

"We're near Galashiels at your Aunty Meredith's." His father spoke quickly. "We can't go back to the estate until the police check it out and say it's safe to secure it."

"I want to be with you guys," he said.

"Try to keep things normal."

"It's bad, isn't it, Dad?"

"Och, I didn't want to worry you, but we've lost a lot with this crash. We should be okay if we sell some of our art. But that depends on what they took from the estate."

"Wh...what are you saying, Dad?"

"Curb your spending. We're in for a hard ride."

Martin double-blinked, clicking his fingers at his side. "But you've got things in reserve, right? Our trust funds are okay, yeah?" A flash of cold crawled up his neck.

"I haven't had a chance to speak to the bank or our accountant yet, what with..." His father exhaled loudly into his phone. "They say it's bad, but people are making it worse withdrawing all their money from the banks and panic buying."

"Tell me about it."

"They say even the Dooms Day Preppers are heading for the hills." His father paused and took another breath. "Go to work. You'll be safe in Edinburgh. I'll keep you posted. I promise."

The unease moved down to Martin's chest as his father disconnected.

Dad was right. He should carry on as normal because *nobody* else was. He lit a cigarette and took a long pull as he left his flat, slamming the door behind him.

Martin walked straight to the nearest supermarket. It was the same there and at the smaller supermarket on the next block—empty shelves from people piling their trolleys with all they could hold. He went to the nearest self-serve deli-food and gourmet-sandwich store and got the last of the pre-packaged sandwiches. About ten in all. He had to think of the next couple of days and there wasn't much else. At the checkout, he tossed some packets of crisps into his basket.

"What's going on?" he asked the girl at the register.

"People are clearing the shelves." She shook her head, eyes wide. "We won't get a delivery in time to restock for tomorrow. At least here they're paying for it. There's been looting, you know."

Martin went back to his flat the long way and stopped at the corner store. He added a carton of cigarettes to his sandwich purchase. Marching home, he hugged his shopping bags close.

This will settle down in a couple of days, right? He lit another cigarette and sucked in.

It had to.

An engine revved as a vehicle coasted close behind him. A sliding van door slammed open, and Martin swung around as footsteps pounded on the pavement. Two guys in black clothing and wearing balaclavas headed right for him, like in some cheesy spy show.

"What the—?" A fist slammed into his guts. "Oof." Pain hit right up into his lungs.

Sandwiches and cigarettes scattered on the footpath. His breath staggered. It went dark as rough cloth covered his face. A ring of pain gripped both his upper arms as they grabbed him and hauled him forward. Martin retaliated, punching out. Pain raged in his knuckles and shot up his arms as his left hand connected with a bony chin, and his right with metal. The sliding van door rumbled open further. One of the men pushed Martin forward onto the hard flooring while another got in beside him, the metal floor echoing with each step.

"Go." The guy had a Glaswegian accent—maybe.

The van skidded off.

"What're you doing?" Martin struggled for air. "Let me go!"

"Shut it!" *Aye, a Glaswegian.*

A boot landed in his back. Hands grabbed him and pulled his arms behind him. The firmness of plastic strips surrounded his wrists and held them together tight. Cutting in.

"Get me out of here!"

Another boot to the back. Martin flinched and caught his breath as intense pain ripped his side.

What? Were they kidnapping him? A chill ran along his spine.

Now? Wonderful bloody timing. When his father has no money. Then the chill settled in his guts. *Will they kill me?*

Martin listened intently, trying to gauge where he was now, and where they were taking him. They travelled out of the suburbs. Never stopping.

"Watch it!" Glaswegian accent yelled at the driver. The van lurched.

"Can't 'elp it. Traffic lights are out." The driver was a cockney. "Looks like they're out everywhere."

"Just get this wee spoilt brat back to the boss in one piece. And us. Aye?"

"Aye, aye, Captain!"

The seat creaked, then there was a slap, like a hand connected with a head.

"Oy! I'm drivin'. Ya not meant to abuse the driver. Okay?"

"Shut up and drive," *Glaswegian* growled.

"Lucky the cops are busy, eh?"

"Not been any around." A younger Scottish voice came from someone sitting beside the Glaswegian.

The traffic sounds and sirens diminished, so they must've driven out of the suburbs. Light filtering through his mask strobed as if they were driving under high lights.

Like on a motorway.

Maybe they were on the motorway, but Martin couldn't tell the direction. Now the hum of the tyres on the road beneath the vehicle changed. The woosh-woosh beside them became regular and close. Passing poles, probably. A seagull squawked. It had to be the bridge over the Firth of Forth. So, they were heading north. That could be anywhere. Stirling, Perth, Dundee, The Highlands even.

Anywhere!

His father would never find him. He needed to escape. If only he'd kept up the Tae Kwon Do.

Chapter Five

Martin estimated they had driven for an hour. Well, the nicotine monsters in his brain were calling for a cigarette, and that usually took about an hour. The van turned off a hard road and travelled down gravel, stones crunching beneath the tyres. It came to a halt. No street lights. Night birds called outside. The door slid open. Rough hands encircled his upper arms and stood him up. The scent of grass and that distinctive odour of the country—cow shit—wafted in his nostrils.

"Out ye get."

He bumped his head on the door frame. "Ow!"

"Watch yer head." *Glaswegian* pushed Martin from behind.

The path wasn't smooth, and Martin stumbled often. A wooden door creaked. A large one. They marched him through to where there was light. The rough material dragged over his eyes and his head was now bare. He shook his hair away from his face and blinked at the light, pain shot through his eyeballs, matching the emerging headache.

The room was wall-to-wall bookshelves, but not all shelves contained books. Ornaments, clocks and dust covered the bookless spaces. A flat screen television sat in front of the bookshelf to the right. The evening news was on the screen with the volume muted. The tickertape at the bottom read *Riots in London, Manchester, and Glasgow.* A smallish man with mousy brown hair and intelligent grey-eyes sat behind the partner's desk in front of Martin. He wore a plain shirt with long sleeves rolled up to the elbows revealing forearms covered in tattoos, and his rapid foot-tapping echoed in the quiet room.

"Welcome. I'm Derrick Lloyd." He stood abruptly and walked around to the front of the desk where his eyes raked Martin from head to foot.

"Tall, aren't you?" Lloyd pursed his lips, his accent a heavy hint of streetwise Glasgow overlaid with some refinement.

"What do you want with me?" Martin pulled at his restrained hands behind his back. The plastic ties remained tight. His palms were damp, joining the moisture in his armpits.

"My plan was to abduct you and hold you for ransom." Steel-grey eyes connected with him. "Then all hell broke loose. But I'm not a man to be put off easily."

"You're holding me for ransom?" Martin couldn't keep the incredulity out of his voice. "But my father's lost his money. He just told me before your—" Martin turned. A solid middle-aged man whose face was permanent *dour*, stood behind him. Must be the Glaswegian. He continued, "associates beat me up and dragged me—"

"That's no concern of mine."

Martin spun back to Lloyd.

"Your father will be able to get what he needs." Lloyd picked up a landline with a handset from the 1980s and made a call. Lloyd listened while it rang. And rang. "Nobody home at your house?"

"My father's not there." Martin glanced around at *Glaswegian* and a younger guy. "We were ransacked. Like I said, he's lost his money."

Lloyd raised an eyebrow and huffed. "We'll try again later."

Martin bit his tongue trying to stop himself from offering his father's mobile number. The family's firm sense of privacy forbade it. But his father would want to be contacted as soon as possible under these circumstances, wouldn't he?

"Phone his mobile." The words spewed out.

"Get his phone." Lloyd flicked his fingers while *Glaswegian* dug in Martin's pockets. He threw his phone to Lloyd. "Hmm. *Daddy*." Lloyd pressed his number. A frown tinged his brow.

"Your phone's dead. Battery's not flat. What's the deal?" Lloyd's gaze bore into Martin while he picked up the handset of the landline and dialled once more.

"I don't know. I spoke to him earlier. Try again." Martin's heart beat up into his throat.

"Declan, try yours." Lloyd lifted his chin to the man behind Martin.

Glaswegian rummaged in his pocket and made a call.

"Mine is nae working either. Mobiles are out the noo, boss," Declan said.

"We shall just have to wait until we can contact *Daddy*. Meanwhile, Declan will show you to your accommodations." Lloyd sniffed. "I chose this place especially."

"You've ransacked it and booted out the owners?" Martin snarled.

His head was beginning to thump. All he needed was a smoke and to get out of here, but neither of those options were going to happen soon.

"No, contrary to popular activity, I didn't ransack this place. I rescued it from abandonment. Not everyone can afford the upkeep of these ageing stately homes. We're not all *new-money,* like your family." Lloyd looked around the room and his mouth curled into a smile.

Martin followed his gaze. Ornate plaster cornices sat up high around the edges and above light fittings.

"Many have had to relinquish homes that have been in their families for generations. I quite like this one." Lloyd shot his stare back to Martin. "You can earn your keep while you're here. Help shore up the defences. I don't want to be a victim like your father, do I?"

Martin clenched his mouth shut.

"Enough chatter. Take him." Lloyd flicked his hand in a dismissive manner.

Declan's massive hands clamped on Martin's arms and dragged him out of the room. The young lad followed. Declan pushed him down the corridor. Martin stumbled past empty rooms, bare floorboards, broken windows and one room that had its outer wall broken and stonework exposed to the elements. He tripped through a door to a large kitchen. A wooden table was the centrepiece, A broken metal strip edged the ancient table top, the nails barely holding it to the timber. A solid fuel stove in a large fireplace was to the side. A second fireplace with a wrought iron structure, which looked like a spit sitting in front of it, was along another wall. He was in a Victorian kitchen, like the one he'd seen at Callendar House, or somewhere like that. His head throbbed.

Why was he giving himself the grand tour?

He cooled with sweat, and his skin crawled in competition with the erratic beats of his heart.

Declan opened a door to the side and shoved him in. Martin landed hard on his right knee, and with his hands still tied behind his back, he fell forward, turning side-on so his shoulder hit the floor.

"Can you at least untie me?" Martin's voice sounded like a shriek in the small room.

It was cool, and wooden shelves ran along the walls either side of him. Wicker baskets and wooden boxes sat stacked on the floor. The pantry then?

Declan came at him with a knife, a sneer cracking the dour face. He spun Martin over and slit the plastic ties.

"Thar ye go, poor wee rich-boy. Hope yer daddy does nae take too long, aye?"

"Don't go gettin' your designer label trousers dirty." The lad at the doorway sniggered.

"Do either of you have a smoke?" Martin asked.

"Not good for your health, ye ken?" the young one said.

The door shut to darkness. Great. No windows. A glow of light came through the crack under the door. Footsteps walked away, the passing shadow of feet a flicker along the bottom edge of the door. He scooted himself backward, so his back was against a wall. Cold seeped through his jacket, now damp on the inside. His father would phone him again tonight and he'd get this all sorted out, right? Lloyd would answer and give his demands. Would his father be able to do it?

Martin scratched at his arms. He really needed a smoke.

He took some deep slow breaths to calm his ragged breathing. His eyes were adjusting. He guessed he was either in Stirling somewhere or in Fife. Yes, Fife had lots of older abandoned buildings in the middle of nowhere. He and Davy had gone standing stone hunting once in the Kingdom of Fife. Ha! He bet Derrick Lloyd thought himself a king—of this castle anyway.

Martin's mind went back to a cigarette. The nicotine monsters were shouting in his head now.

Wow, it has barely been two hours.

He coughed over a dry mouth. It was going to be a long night. In the darkness, he'd not know when it was daybreak. He laid down on the floor, curled in a ball and grabbed his jacket tight, and settled in for a night of fighting his demons.

Chapter Six

Night time didn't get any better and by morning the demon-monster nicotine-demanding crazies were roaring in Martin's brain. He dry-retched and rolled over, his fingers tingling. He opened his eyes. The light coming from under the door was stronger and lit the pantry. Martin stood. And paced. Then stomped to the old wooden door and pounded.

"Let me out!"

Silence.

"Hey! Lemme out!" He strode around the confines of the Victorian pantry.

The door flew open, and sunlight poured in.

"Shut it!" Declan's solid frame crowded the doorway; his brow furrowed, and his mouth turned down in a permanent snarl.

"Have you got a cigarette I could have? Please?" Martin cringed at the begging in his tone.

Declan's face almost split apart with a smile. If that's what it was.

"No."

Martin closed his eyes and swallowed down what little saliva his mouth produced.

"I need to pee. You're gonna let me pee, aren't you?"

Declan reached forward and grabbed him by the jacket. He dragged him down a different corridor to a bathroom and pushed him in. The toilet was an older style with a cistern high on the wall with a chain hanging from it. Martin stepped to the stained wooden seat then turned his head.

"You gonna stand there while I pee?"

"Aye."

"But I also need to..."

Declan tilted his head. "Crap?"

Martin nodded.

"Och weel, being a rich-boy, your shite will nae stink, will it? So, I'll have nae inconveniences while I stand here for that, will I then?" Declan's face cracked his version of a smile once more.

After Martin did what he needed to do, Declan marched him back to the pantry. Martin slid his gaze to the scene behind the estate house. His burning face forgotten as he began to gather data. Green fields skirted undulating hills. Farmlands, patchworked with different crops, filled the views framed by broken window-work.

Aye, Fife.

Down the passageway the aroma of frying bacon made his stomach turn.

Declan shoved him into the pantry and followed with a plate of food he'd picked up from the kitchen table, then left shutting the pantry door behind him. Martin tried to eat but the roaring in his brain was now in his stomach and even holding the plate of bacon and eggs convulsed his stomach. He placed the plate of barely touched food by the door and leaned back, breathing deeply, sweat trickling down his face.

The murmur of voices came from the kitchen.

Martin stood and thumped on the door. "Declan!"

"Aye." Declan opened the door. "I'd wish it to be known that I'm nae pleased to be on a first name basis with ye. What do ye want?"

"I'd like to know if my father has phoned."

"No."

"So, mobiles are still out?" He'd get what he needed from this guy, whatever it took.

Declan slid his phone out of his trouser pocket and tried a number. "No. Mines works."

"So, will Derrick try my father again?"

"Mr Lloyd to you." Declan turned and left the room, leaving the pantry door ajar.

The younger man sat at the long wooden table eating breakfast. The wrought iron stove roared with its fire within, and heat seeped through into the pantry.

"Ye should have eaten, for today you'll begin your work, ken," the young guy said.

"What work?" Martin's brow tensed.

"Like Mr Lloyd said. 'Shorin' up the defences.' You're going to build a wall." The young guy shoved another fork-full of fried egg into his mouth. "That'll get those designer trousers o' yours dirty now, will it no'?" He laughed around the yellow egg.

Declan strode over to the pantry.

"Well, if ye are no' eatin'." Declan dragged Martin by the collar and marched him outside to a pile of stonework.

He made Martin carry the blocks of cut stone, one at a time, to the area beside the broken wall of the house. It was heavy work but at least it took Martin's mind off his cravings. Martin's arms shook and focusing was difficult at times. Lunch was a sandwich which he ate and kept down. Declan and *young guy* stood and watched. A handgun stuck out of Declan's belt. He pushed his jacket aside to reveal it whenever Martin glanced in his direction.

Walking back and forth to the pile of stone bricks, Martin scanned the surrounding countryside as far as he could see. At the back of the stately home stood a farmhouse way off in the distance over exposed fields. No drystone walls or hedgerows, except far off near what could be a road, and the nearest trees were far away at the base of some hills. They would easily see him if he ran that way.

"Keep your eye on your work, rich boy," Declan growled.

Martin stood in front of Declan, the cut stone block he held dragging on his arms. Sweat stuck his shirt to his back. He tightened his mouth and narrowed his eyes at his captors.

Declan raised his brow and placed his hand on the stock of his handgun.

"You're imprisoning me!" Martin stood over Declan as he spoke into the harsh face.

The minder tightened his grip on his handgun and leaned forward, their noses now inches apart.

"You're being held for ransom." Declan's rough whisper accompanied his stale breath.

Martin held his mouth closed and marched to the house where his pile of bricks grew, conscious of Declan's eyes boring into his back.

The wall that needed repair was a couple of layers deep. He did some quick calculations for the amount of brickwork involved, gauging from the size of the cut stone that remained in the wall. Most of it was rubble and it required new, decent stone. It wasn't the kind of thing you bought at a hardware store. In his calculations, he allowed for what seemed to be a window, and the gradual narrowing of the stone bricks as the wall rose to join the existing stonework, and then on up to the roof. Its repair was no simple task and the amount of cut stone already obtained, according to his calculations, wouldn't be near enough. The wind picked up behind him and blew straight into the room.

"You'll need a stonemason to fix that wall." Martin threw the observation at Declan while he passed empty handed on his way back to the pile of cut stone. Declan snarled and continued his mumbled conversation with *young guy*.

At the pile, Martin walked straight on. Turning left was the driveway. He kicked himself into action and ran hard down the narrow gravel road. His thighs burned, and every muscle screamed.

Curses came from behind him.

The driveway led to a bitumen road. Martin pounded down it. Lungs burning, heart thundering. This was his chance. Declan and *young guy's* shouts rose from near the house.

Martin turned right down a sideroad with houses in the distance. Maybe a small village. A lorry approached. Martin waved wildly. His heart thudded in relief as the lorry skidded to a halt.

"What 'ave we got 'ere, matey?" Cockney jumped down from the driver's side.

Hands as solid as iron grabbed him from behind and spun him around. Declan came into view for a moment, face contorted. Then a fist of knuckles connected with Martin's eye and the world blurred.

"Wee eejit!"

Martin fell to the ground, hard bitumen smacking the other side of his face. Boots pelted his back. Pain rose along with bile, burning his throat and mingling with his groans.

Declan hauled him up and marched him back to the grounds of the house. Martin's face pulsated, and his vision diminished as his left eyelid started swelling.

"That was a stupid move." Declan shook him.

Young guy laughed.

"Keep movin' those stones, laddie." Declan's breath filled Martin's nostrils.

More stomach heaving. Fingers grabbed his hair and pulled his head back. His skin, now tight at the sides, sent shots of pain into his swollen eye.

"Ye still have work tae do," Declan growled into his ear as he pushed him forward to the pile of cut masonry.

Vans and lorries arrived on and off throughout the day, close to where Martin picked up the stones. Goods and supplies filled each vehicle and Lloyd's men carried boxes, cartons, and tubs into the house.

By evening, Martin's limbs were heavy, his headache continuous and his left eye swollen shut. He drank the whole flask of water *young guy* handed him on entering the kitchen. The far wall of the kitchen now had stacks of boxes sitting against it. *Young guy* pushed him into the pantry and shut the door. Its shelves were full of goods, and sacks full of flour, rice and other similar foodstuffs crowded the floor. The smell of fish and cooking oil wafted under the door. Martin's stomach turned only slightly. The door opened, and *young guy* placed a plate of fish and chips on the floor.

"Eat the food of the common folk." *Young guy* sat back at the kitchen table next to Declan and watched Martin through the open door.

"I'm not royalty, you know?" Martin leaned forward. "You've picked the wrong hostage if that's what you're thinking."

"Shut it, rich boy." Declan's dour face came into view in the door frame. "We don't want to put up with your *greetin'* for any longer than we have to."

"I'm not just a rich kid, you know."

"Your daddy will be poor by the time Mr Lloyd and this crash have finished with him."

"I'm studying to be a physicist," Martin said. "What contribution to humankind are *you* making?"

"Uni student, are ye now? Well, ye will nae be that for long either. Have ye seen what's goin' on oot there?"

"No, because you've locked me in a cupboard!"

Martin sat back and ate. His lack-of-nicotine headache seemed slightly less after food, but it remained. So did the face-pain around his eye. And the sting from the grazes on the other side of his face. Then a familiar scent wafted over from the table. Martin jerked his head in that direction.

Declan sat at the long wooden table, hand to mouth, holding a cigarette and pulling hard. The end glowed a red inferno. Declan blew out the smoke, aiming in Martin's direction. Martin's hands itched, his shoulders tensed, and his monsters screamed once more. He stood and, snapping his fingers by his side, scooted the empty plate out the door. It skidded to a halt at one of the heavy legs of the kitchen table. He slammed the door to the pantry.

Martin flung his back hard against the door, mouth dry but body drenched in sweat. Fingers tingling. He coughed and took some deep breaths to ease the churn in his stomach. When were they going to contact his father? Or maybe they had, and he was finding ways of getting the cash. How much had Derrick Lloyd demanded?

Someone pounded on the door as he lent against it, vibrating his entire body. Then it began to open, shoving him forward.

"Move!" Declan shouted. "The boss wants ye."

Chapter Seven

"Ciao, bella." Mario strode past Shona, holding a tray high over the restaurant patrons; steam rose from bowls of pasta drowned in his mama's spaghetti sauce. It was a family affair, this little Italy in the middle of Edinburgh.

"Ciao yourself, *Romeo*." Shona's mouth tugged to the side as she passed Mario on her way out to the kitchen. Stopping a grin was impossible around this gorgeous man.

Oh, but there is something about Italian men.

Shona shook her head slightly. He mustn't distract her again this shift. Her waitressing job was great. She loved the vibrancy. The colour. The *family* of Italian dining. Food and *La Famiglia* were so important to her bosses. And so different from home. Shona pushed her disappointment at her own parents aside and tied the cute uniform apron around her waist.

"You enjoy your *dimostrazione* last night, bella?" Mario strode into the kitchen with an empty tray under his arm. The deep-brown eyes in the olive-skinned face with the dark six o'clock-shadowed chin were knee-melting. "You find another cause for this week?"

"What?" Shona picked up the tablet. "That protest outside of Scottish Parliament was important." A flicker of annoyance flashed through her. "Are you sayin' I'm not genuine?"

Mario put his hand over his heart. "No, bella. I'm a saying, you need to choose *Uno*." He held up a finger. "You cannot fight the cause for everyone, no?"

"Have you seen what's going on out there?"

"*Si*. Business is down," Joey called from the cooker. Steam surrounded him, and delicious aromas of garlic and spices flowed from his direction. The restaurant's pantry was full to overflowing for Joey had ensured the business was well stocked. The minute things started going sideways, he and Shona had shopped at a local wholesaler. They'd had two trolleys each, which Joey filled with food and other goods.

"All o' dis"—Joey waved his hands around widely— "it scares the *turisti* and everybody else."

"Can I leave early then?" Shona asked her boss. "There's another rally in front of Parliament this afternoon. I'd like to be there."

Joey shrugged and held both hands palm up, screwing his mouth to the side. "It's a your money you don't a make if you leave early, *si*?"

"Well, if it's quiet we'll finish early so...?"

"I'll be fine, bella." Mario stepped to the servery and put the plates of tagliatelle, topped with prawns swimming in garlic butter, on his tray. "You go save the world from this present crisis."

Shona walked along South St David Street, Edinburgh. She'd lose wages leaving work early but there were more important things to think about.

Aye, if the people didn't call the Government and the banks to account, then no one would have jobs or money.

She reached Princes Street. It was still a mess from the other night. The employees of those large stores had cleared the broken glass and rubbish left by the looters. Now the storefronts were boarded up. She kept walking straight ahead and cut through Princes Street Park, an oasis of green quiet.

Once on the Mile, she turned left and made her way down to the Scottish Parliament building. Its modern styled lines and smooth sandstone walls always made her heart swell. Scotland was modern and progressive, keeping up with Europe. The quotations on the stone walls and the pavement out front reflected Scotland's past and the passion of its people.

What was Mario on about? This was nae a *cause for the week*. This was Scotland's cause, and she was about to join her voice with other Scots. The banks had shafted them all again and everyone should be raging at them and the government.

The crowd had spilled onto the street, the same as the other night. Shona drew closer and a muffled voice echoed out of the megaphone. A line of clear shields and police in riot gear made a barrier behind the demonstrators who stood on the road and around the shallow water-features in front of the parliament building. The vibe was different this afternoon. Instead of the unity and openness of expression belonging to the previous demonstration, there was a tinge of fear in the air. The line of black uniforms behind the tall, clear, polycarbonate-wall of riot shields, made people nervous. Police on horses flanked the front-guard, their mounts nickering.

"The Government is nae answering us." The man with the megaphone spoke up above the unsettled grumblings of the crowd in front of him. "They're draggin' their feet, so they are. They need to tell us what they're goin' tae do aboot it all, aye?"

The crowd replied with shouts of agreement, all mixing together to make one loud, angry response. Horses stirred as cannisters flew into the crowd. The smoke released and spread through the body of the rally. People coughed and they moved away *en mass* from the source of the smoke. The line of clear shields pushed further in.

Shona's heart came into her throat. This could only end badly. She spun and manoeuvred her way out of the crowd, thankful she had only made it to the edge at the front.

"Quick, come this way!" a guy in jeans shouted. Shona and those standing near her followed him up the Mile and along a narrow street as others from the crowd ran past the entrance to the street, tear gas swirling and following their escape. Shouting rose to an uproar as more people ran and horses' hooves clattered up the Mile after them. Sweat trickled down Shona's back inside her orange work blouse.

"Follow me! I ken a way out." The guy in jeans led Shona and the others who followed, further into the lane where a side road exited. Shona was on this guy's heels, needing to get out of there.

No way would they catch and arrest her.

A sharp turn brought them to a narrower lane, which came to a sudden end. A van parked at the exit with its side door open. The guy who'd led them to it turned and grabbed Shona, while another man from the van jumped out and seized a young man who had followed close all the way. Yelps and clatter of the others running to escape the abductors receded behind them.

Shona screamed. The guy who'd grabbed her tied a piece of cloth so it covered her mouth. She kicked, and he grunted, tugging harder on the rag-bit in her mouth. He used it to manoeuvre her against the van where he tied her hands behind her back.

"Hey! You can't do this." The young man who'd followed with her shouted at their abductors as they dragged his hands behind his back.

Shona's vision went dark as the guy who'd manhandled her pulled a bag over her head. He shoved her forward. She landed hard on the floor of the van, knees stinging. The young man captured with her landed beside her and grunted.

"You can't do—" His voice muffled.

"Be quiet, both of ye."

Shona kicked out, not caring what she hit. Her shin thudded on a seat post and her breath almost left her. Her foot connected with something soft and podgy, and the young man next to her grunted.

"Settle down." The command came with a sharp slap to her thigh. Strong hands crossed her feet at the ankles and wrapped tape around them.

"We needed more than two," one of her abductors said.

"Well, the others ran before we could get 'em," the other replied.

"We'll get more another time."

Temples thudding and icy guts churning, Shona focused on managing her breathing and paying attention to the sounds and scents of her journey.

I'm going to get out of this!

Chapter Eight

Declan marched Martin along the corridor, his hand grasping Martin's jacket by the collar. Martin glanced to his left. The rooms now stored boxes, tubs, and crates. They were on the other side of the house. He caught the view through the front windows. In the near distance was the road on which the vans and lorries had arrived, and more farmlands with white-washed cottages dotted here and there. Further behind those, the grey-blue of a body of water ran to the horizon. If he recalled his Scottish geography correctly, it was the wider section of the Firth of Forth where it led out to sea. That area of Fife would be the way to go when he tried again.

More cover. More people to help him.

"Eyes front." Declan shook him, sending Martin's vision blurry.

The throbbing in his eye continued. Declan stopped him before a familiar door, then knocked.

"Come," Lloyd called from within the library.

Declan opened the door and pushed Martin in.

"Tried to escape, did we?" Lloyd grasped the book in front of him, his knuckles whitening.

Martin breathed in, nostrils flaring. He wasn't going to answer. He glanced at the silent television that displayed footage of a crowd teeming through tear gas while the army in riot gear sprayed them with high-pressure hoses. Smoke surrounded the tall pillar of Nelson's Column and people clambered over bronze lions.

"Yes. Troubles down south. And most other cities in this great United Kingdom, including my beloved Glasgow." Lloyd rose from his seat and walked to stand in front of his desk. "In fact, most major cities of the world are experiencing the same unrest."

Martin drew his eyes away from the flat screen television.

"Small businesses are folding," Lloyd continued. "Some of the larger ones already have. Amazon, that giant, gone…" Lloyd flicked his fingers in a puff-of-smoke gesture. "Banks are reclaiming houses. Suddenly middle-class families are becoming street dwellers." He leaned forward. "And what is the Government doing? Sending in the military to sort out the rabble. Wasting the taxpayer's money shoring up the banks."

Martin glanced back to the screen. Full rubbish bags sat around garbage bins lining a suburban street. *Local government services halted as unpaid staff strike*, the tickertape read at the bottom of the screen. *Power outages expected to be more frequent.*

"The world is changing. The old order is out. The New Order, in. Medieval times once more, my friend. I'm the laird and you're the serf. No, not even that. The once high and mighty son-of-a-rich-man is now this poor bastard's slave." Lloyd pointed to himself. "Aye, my parents were druggies. I dragged myself up. Lived on the streets, became part of a gang." He cocked his head. "Then led the gang. Educated myself." He thrust his index finger onto his desk. "Now I will live here in my fortification. People will come to *me* for what they need."

"What?" Martin could barely get the question out.

"Hmm." Lloyd tilted his head and frowned. "And I seem to be having difficulty getting in contact with Kieran Moffatt, electronics magnate."

Panic flared in Martin's mind. "What're you going to do with me?"

"You'll get your hands dirty rebuilding my wall. No more university, books and theoreticals for you. It's practical work and being at my beck-and-call until your father pays up."

"What if you can't contact him? What if—?"

"Well, then you're mine for keeps, *slave*." Lloyd's grin held no friendship as he waved him out.

Declan grabbed Martin's collar with his fist then shoved him along toward the kitchen. Shouts and the clamour of scuffles came down the corridor—a young woman's voice among the hollering.

"Quieten down, now. What's going on in here?" Declan's voice bellowed past Martin's ears, leaving them ringing.

Young guy pushed a person into the pantry and slammed the door.

"Some 'elpers for rich-boy." Cockney was back. He'd driven the van in and out all day.

Declan thrust Martin aside, still holding his collar, and turned Martin to face him.

"We've found some fellow slaves to work with you. Play nice, now." Declan inclined his head to the pantry door as *young guy* opened it. "In!" Declan shoved.

Martin stumbled in and fell over someone's extended legs. He turned. He'd recognise that hedgehog hairstyle anywhere—*Davy!*

"Martin? What happened to your eye?"

"What are *you* doing here?" *Man, what's it got like out there?*

"I was mugged. They threw me in the van...with her." Davy pointed to a young woman squatting against the boxes on the opposite wall. Her dark hair hung over her makeup smeared face. Her trousers and orange top were lower-end High Street. Dark-brown eyes bore into his.

"What's going on?" Her rough Wester Hailes' accent rang out.

"Ah...we are here to work." Martin wasn't going to tell the whole story. His pals at the café were unaware of who his father was, and he'd always tried to keep it that way.

"We were abducted to *work*?" The young woman's brows rose. "Against our will? That's ridiculous!" She stood and stepped past Martin to the door which she then pounded with both fists. "Let us out! This is kidnap!"

The door burst open. Stepping back, the young woman tripped over Martin and landed heavily on the hard stone floor.

"Ooh!" Davy grabbed for her, failing in his attempt to break her fall.

"Oy! Rich kid." Cockney stabbed Martin with his glare. "Keep yer fellow slaves in line. Okay?"

Martin glared back, biting down the vitriol threatening to spew out. The door slammed shut.

"Are you alright?" Davy patted the young woman's arm. She flicked him away, got up and returned to the opposite wall.

Davy rubbed his hands. Then looked at Martin. "Rich kid?"

Martin swallowed. *Damn.* What would it matter now if Davy knew?

"I don't really know why you guys are here, but I'm being held for ransom."

Davy screwed up his face. "No." He shook his head and his stomach vibrated with silent laughter. Then he opened his mouth and let it out.

"It's not funny." Martin couldn't keep the annoyance out of his tone. "I'm dead serious."

Davy's laughter filled the small pantry.

A fist banged on the door. "Shut it!"

Davy put his hands over his mouth and gradually suppressed his laughter.

"Who's yer father?" The brown eyes in the far corner hit him with a direct stare.

"My father is Kieran Moffatt."

"Who's he when he's about?" she asked.

"Moffatt Electronics?" Davy's eyes were wide. "He's your father? You're his son?"

"That's usually how it goes, Einstein." The young woman had crouched low against the wall.

"How did you get mugged? I thought you were pretty streetwise, Davy." Martin flicked a glance at the woman opposite, not wanting to voice his opinion of her street cred.

"Martin, it's really bad out there." Davy grabbed Martin's arm. "People are rioting and...the place is a mess. I was on my way back from work and got caught up in a demonstration. Darren's had to close. I helped him board up the shop. They've been looting the Royal Mile!" Davy's voice rose a pitch.

The woman coughed. Martin turned to her. "What's your name?"

"Shona. And I've nae body who could pay a ransom for *me*." Her mouth became a thin line. "But I'll get out o' here. I'm no' stayin'."

"You'll never get past those guys," Davy whispered. He looked at Martin's face then glanced down at his dusty trousers. "What work have you been doing?"

"Manual labour. Derrick Lloyd wants to fix—"

"Who's he?" Shona asked.

"The boss. Thinks he's the laird of the mansion," Martin scoffed.

"What's all this stuff then?" Shona tapped the box next to her. "Someone's been busy looting."

"Part of Lloyd's plan," Martin said. "He's going to sell it."

"People'll want it," Davy observed. "The shops are empty. The storehouses are getting that way too. Some factories have shut down...temporarily, or so they say."

"Setting up his own wee empire." Shona opened the box next to her.

"Don't do that." Martin held his hand out to stop her.

Shona continued to open it.

"Stop." Martin stepped over to her. "They're not nice guys. They won't like it."

"Well, I'm hungry," she said as she rummaged. "Jars of spaghetti sauce. Do they feed you here?"

"Aye, but I think dinner's over."

Shona opened another box. This time she found cheese sticks. "That's more like it."

She handed some to Davy who hesitated, but then took three and ate them. Shona held out some to Martin. He shook his head.

"I've eaten." Martin settled his back against the wall.

Visions of Declan's dour face snarling at him came to him in his dreams throughout the night.

Chapter Nine

Davy leaned against Martin. The snoring had started in the early hours when Martin woke after cigarette-deprived nightmares. The screaming crazies demanding nicotine had eased but sleeping was still difficult. Now the rhythmic passage of air past Davy's slightly collapsed airways was the regular reminder that Martin was *not* asleep.

Martin looked over at Shona, the early morning daylight was just enough to see her. She seemed peaceful as she lay with her head on her hands. She'd have a stiff neck when she woke. She wasn't pretty; she was rough around the edges but seemed smart.

Martin was used to being with attractive people, like Caitlin. Had they found her? He had no way of knowing. A heaviness centred on his chest. He hoped she wasn't alone and scared, wherever she was.

Maybe today he'd hear that Lloyd had contacted his father and the money was on its way. His father would find a way to get it despite the banks closing, and thugs ransacking their house, and—

Davy let rip a pig-snorting snore, then snapped awake. "What? What d'you say?"

"Nothing." Martin glanced over at Shona.

The snore-of-the-century had woken her too.

Davy dozed off again.

"Hi," Martin whispered.

"Hi, yourself."

"Did you sleep okay?"

"Aye, until blubber-boy snored." Shona straightened her crumpled orange shirt.

"He's been snoring from the wee hours."

"We're in Fife, aren't we?" she asked.

"Aye, that's what I thought." He kept his voice soft and pointed to the front of the house. "Coast is that way."

"I used to come here to ma grannie's house for summer holidays. I got a feeling we're near Kirkcaldy."

"Aye, I think you're right."

"What do ye do, apart from being a rich brat? Mind you, ye dinnae seem like a rich brat. You're smart, aren't you? You sound like it from the way ye speak. And you have a look on yer face like your mind is always working."

"That's because it is," he said.

The door flung open. "If you're awake, ye can work."

"What?" Davy snorted awake.

"Out, all o' ye." Dour-faced Declan stared down at them. "You have a fence to build."

"What about the house wall?" Martin asked.

"Well, as ye so rightly pointed out, *physicist*, it requires the expertise of a stonemason. And well, they're not too happy about coming out this way at present. So, it's fence building for you all today."

Martin stood and stretched. The others followed as he walked behind Declan to the front of the house. The edge of the world glowed orange as clouds over the Firth pinked and touched the water with magenta. The air was crisp and the fragrance of cow not too overpowering. Perhaps he was getting used to it.

Martin turned and took in the view. Birds chattered in the far trees. There was no traffic on the road near the farms to the south. A solid object thudded against his spine. Martin spun.

"Shovels today." Declan thrust the handle of the implement into Martin's hand and gave one each to Shona and Davy. Declan walked ahead to where a long piece of string was tied to stakes along the front of the house. He paced certain intervals and, with a spray can, marked the ground with orange paint.

"Dig."

They each went to an orange spot and began. During the next hour, they got a turn at going to the bathroom to respond to nature's call, under supervision. Shona came back stony-faced with *young guy* trailing behind her. Then Declan allowed them a break and they went inside for a breakfast of cereal.

The day wore on and a light drizzle became rain as the sky greyed over with the clouds and the rain the sunrise had promised. Shona's top was wet. Martin stopped his digging and removed his jacket and handed it to her.

"Nae thanks. I would nae mind a real designer label, but it stinks." Droplets fell from the strands of hair hanging over her forehead. "I'd rather stay wet than be mingin' of your B.O."

"Please yourself."

"Why a fence? We couldn't run with these minders."

Martin flicked a glance at Declan and *young guy*. "They're in for the long haul. Lloyd is building an empire on the back of disaster, so he thinks."

Shona frowned and kept digging.

They dug a decent hole each and pounded posts in with a post-driver. The rain became heavier in the afternoon, the surrounding air thick with moisture and the view now a green and white monochrome. The patter against water-soaked ground was a constant background noise. Declan ensured the posts were aligned and perpendicular. Then Martin and the others went in, their worksite now a quagmire.

"I need a shower." Shona stood in front of Declan, her face streaked with dirt and her clothes mud-stained. "With some privacy. No perverts observing this time, okay?"

Declan's eyes narrowed. "Verra well."

"Ah, may I have one also?" Davy asked.

"Aye." Declan squeaked his voice and waggled his head. "Ye may have one also." He turned to Martin. "I suppose you want one too, rich boy? Although, I should nae be calling you that anymore, as *Daddy's* not come up with the goods yet."

Martin's feet stuck to the floor as ice ran down his spine already cold from his damp clothing.

"You haven't got him?"

"Oh aye, we've got him. Just no' got any money from him." Declan pouted. "Maybe you're not worth as much to him as ye thought."

Shona gasped.

"He's just finding the money in difficult circumstances." Martin blinked.

"Better have not got the police involved," Declan growled.

"Police are too busy," Davy piped up. "More important things to bother about. Like the world falling apart."

"Anyway, slaves, if ye want your showers, get going to the bathroom." Declan pointed down the hallway.

Young guy followed them.

"What's that young guy's name?" Shona whispered over her shoulder as Martin walked behind her.

"Don't know."

"Don't leave me alone with him. Please."

"Okay." He stretched the word out. "You mean, you want me to shower with you?"

"No," she exclaimed over her shoulder. "Just be around if he decides to be there."

Martin showered and put back on his damp, dirty clothes and stood near the doorway while Davy and Shona took their turn in the shower.

Young guy hung around the open bathroom door.

"Clean clothes would have been nice." Martin stepped in front of their minder when he leaned into the bathroom.

He scowled as Martin blocked his view. "It is nae a hotel, slave."

Young guy escorted them back to the kitchen. Food preparation for dinner had not yet begun. Martin's stomach grumbled.

"Are we getting to eat tonight?" Davy asked Declan when he ushered them into the pantry.

"Aye." Shona pointed at the open boxes. "You've enough to make a nice pasta here."

"What have ye been doing?" Declan yelled.

Silence filled the pantry.

"Have you been into the stores?"

"I, well, just had a wee look." Shona remained by the boxes.

"They are nae yours to look at!" Declan bellowed.

He stepped into the pantry and grabbed Shona's arm. Her eyes widened.

"It was all of us," Martin said.

"No, it was just *me*." Shona gave Martin a dagger-eyed look.

"Come here." Declan dragged her out of the pantry and down the passageway to the library. *Young guy* sniggered and slammed the door in Martin's face.

"Shit!" Davy said.

"Shit, alright. Didn't I tell you two to leave their stuff alone?" Martin's heart raced.

Davy squatted against the wall, chewing his nails.

Martin clicked his fingers by his thigh. "If they question us, we were all in it, okay?"

"Why?" Davy asked, his question muffled around his fingers in his mouth.

"It'll make it harder for them to punish us."

Davy pulled his hands away from his lips. "Why?"

"If they hurt all their *slaves*, they won't get any work done, will they?"

Faint yelling drifted down the hallway. Then a yelp. Footsteps approached the kitchen. Two sets. Then the pantry door flew open. Declan, who had returned Shona to the kitchen where she stood with her back to them, now stormed into the pantry, grabbed jars of spaghetti sauce, paused at the open box of cheese strips, cursed at the obviously used and empty packaging, and stormed out, leaving the door open.

Shona placed a large pot on the stove and tipped water from a jug into it.

"You're cooking for twelve tonight." Declan threw packets of mince onto the table next to the jars of sauce.

"Aye." Shona didn't look at Declan while she turned and got a frying pan down from the hanging rack and placed it on the stove. Her face was blotched red, a darkening developing on her right cheek.

"Have you bastards hit her?" Martin couldn't keep it in.

"Shut it, or you'll be next. And we don't pull our punches, as you well ken!"

"It's okay, Martin." Shona's voice was thin. "I'm cooking us some dinner."

"You shut it and cook," Declan shouted at Shona as he stormed to the pantry door and slammed it in Martin's face.

Chapter Ten

Two weeks passed, and Martin's routine was set. Fence building. Fence building, and more fence building. Still nothing from his father, that they'd told him of anyway. Dour-faced Declan remained his cheery self but at least Shona's cooking was something to look forward to at the end of a long day of post digging.

"So, you cooked in the Italian restaurant?" Davy's bowl muffled his voice.

He leaned against the pantry wall after their day of hard labour, licking the juices remaining from his meal.

"Aye. Well, no. I did nae cook for the customers, like. But Joey, the chef, taught me at the end of the shift sometimes when we had a chance and the staff needed feedin'." Shona smiled and her face lit up.

Martin gulped. He'd judged her too harshly at first. She was a rough Wester Hailes lass, but clever and resourceful. And brave. So much more than her postcode suggested. She'd stared down *young guy* when he'd ogled her. That was becoming more frequent. Her accent still grated on him, but she spoke with a passion when it came to the state of the world and what should be done about it. Her view was a simplistic one of a complex problem, but at least she'd considered it, and had tried to do something about it. That's what had got her here.

Shona leaned to her left and brought out an object from behind the box that held tins of tuna.

"I've managed to get us a little something. They'll no notice it's missin' as I'm the one who does the cookin'," she whispered and held up the large steel cooking spoon.

Martin blinked.

"We can sharpen it," Shona mouthed and did a mime of rubbing it to a point on a stone wall.

An engine pulled up near the back door. Men's voices and murmurings choked by gags, came through the door with the footsteps of new captives.

Martin looked at Shona and Davy, putting a finger to his lips as the group passed the closed pantry door. The heavy footsteps of Lloyd's men trod next to lighter steps of high heels clicking on wooden floors. They marched down the corridor and clattered into a room further on. Footsteps came back to the pantry door. It opened.

"Right chef, out." *Young guy* held the door and snapped his fingers at Shona. "Need food for the new arrivals."

Shona got up and took the dirty plates out to the kitchen and started preparing a meal.

"Who are they?" Martin asked when their jailer began closing the door.

"None 'o your business." The door was half-shut. "But let's just say, they will nae be diggin' holes, ken?" He sniggered and he closed the door fully.

"What does he mean?" Davy frowned.

Martin shrugged. The noise of a busy kitchen resumed as Shona worked her magic there. Declan's growled orders as he settled in the new arrivals, travelled along the corridor.

"Go away." Shona's voice came to Martin even though the door remained closed. Fear tinged her usual bravado.

Martin stood on tiptoes. High up on the pantry door was a crack he'd found and if he stretched, he could see out. Shona had her back to the stove, a pan of water on to boil. *Young guy* stood facing her, his back to Martin. He towered over Shona whose eyes widened and her mouth tensed. Her hands came up trying to hold him away. He lurched forward, pushing Shona away from the stove and up against the boxes by the wall, his head buried in her neck. Shona opened her mouth to scream.

"Leave her alone!" Martin shouted at the door. His voice beat back at him.

Young guy ignored Martin and covered Shona's mouth with one hand, and grabbed her breast with the other. Shona's scream stifled beneath his hand.

"What's happening?" Davy's strangled voice came from behind Martin.

Heat coursed through Martin's veins as burning centred in his throat. He spun, scanning the room for an implement to open the door. Shouldering it would be useless because it opened inward. The metal spoon's handle stuck out slightly from its hiding place behind the box of tuna.

"Martin?" Davy's voice was panicked-question.

In the kitchen, Shona continued to scream behind her assailant's hand.

Martin grabbed the metal spoon and angled it into the door to prize it open. He pushed and levered but it didn't budge. Davy grunted. Behind Martin, he smashed an old wooden crate. Martin placed the spoon handle right next to the ancient Victorian lock, in between the lock and the door jamb. He pushed, levering the door toward him. Davy slipped a chock of wood in the gap. The gap stayed open. Martin nodded and dug his metal-spoon lever into the wood behind the strike plate. He'd noted the state of the aged door jamb previously. Maybe it would break in its weakened state. He pressed hard again. The door flung open and splinters of wood flew; the lock and strike plate still connected.

Shona's muffled screams held anger. Grunts of effort came from her and the young man as she tugged at his hair and clothing, trying to push him away.

Martin strode forward and grabbed *young guy* by the scruff of the neck. He pulled him off Shona then flung him against the kitchen table, face down. Martin lifted his arm high. He aimed his elbow with all his weight behind him, thudding it down onto *young guy's* back. Right between his shoulder blades. A winded grunt came from the young man sprawled across the table.

"What in the bloody hell's going on?" Declan's voice echoed in the kitchen as he entered, scanning the room. His gaze fell on Shona crying behind Martin and flicked to Davy standing in the broken doorway of the pantry. His glare flashed on his assistant sprawled on the kitchen table, then slid to Martin.

"You!" His heavy steps came toward Martin. "Git here!" Declan grabbed him by the collar. Skin pinched where his grasp included flesh. Declan hauled him to Lloyd's door, Martin's feet dragging down the corridor behind him.

"But Shona! Don't leave her with that *creep*," Martin gasped.

Lloyd's door opened.

"Can you not keep a handle on your charges, Declan?" Napoleon's double stood in the doorway.

"Please don't let him touch her," Martin said right into the little man's face.

Lloyd cocked an eyebrow at Declan. "Deal with it."

Declan thrust Martin into the library and shut the door. His footsteps receded, and yelling ensued in the kitchen.

"Sit!" Lloyd stood by a bookshelf and glared at Martin.

Martin shuffled to the nearest chair and sat. Thudding footsteps made their way to a room further along from the kitchen. A door slammed. More yelling, then Declan returned.

"Sorted?" Lloyd growled.

"Aye, Mr Lloyd. But I have to deal with the troublemakers."

"Who are?" Lloyd's tone was as though he barely held his temper in check.

"This one." Declan sneered at Martin. "And one of our own."

"Who?" Lloyd snapped.

"Sean."

Lloyd closed his eyes and took a breath. "You'll have to reprimand him."

"Aye, boss."

"If he can't keep his hands off the fish-wife, then I can't trust him with the merchandise."

Declan looked at the floor. "I'll speak to him, boss."

"He behaves, or he goes. I don't care *whose* nephew he is."

"Aye, boss."

"Attend to this"—Lloyd gestured to Martin— "as you see fit but don't kill him. Daddy's possibly coming through."

Martin lifted his head, his heartbeat kicking up a notch. "You've contacted—?"

"Shut it, you!" Declan grabbed his shirt collar and dragged him off the chair and out of the room, then down to the kitchen. Sean sat by the table looking sorry for himself, and cockney stood over the stove, stirring the pot of stew Shona had started.

Declan thrust Martin's face down onto the kitchen table, the whole length of his upper torso contacting the wood. Hollow, breathless pain erupted below his chest bone. Declan strode around the table to Sean.

"Last chance, *chancer*. Then you're 'oot!" Declan slapped Sean on the side of the head.

Martin made to stand.

"Stay where ye are. Face down." Declan continued his walk around the table. "Some good old-fashioned punishment would nae go astray here in this good old-fashioned kitchen." The clicking of a belt unbuckling and the sliding of leather through loops were the only sounds.

"You two! One on each arm. Hold him down."

The two men obeyed, and they soon pulled Martin's arms apart. His chest muscles burned with the stretch, and his face pressed into the wooden table. The rough metal-edging dug into his wrists where the men pressed his hands down hard on either side of the table. The scent of something musty and rancid filled his nostrils and the hardwood pinched his cheek where the last tenderness of a bruise surrounded his eye.

Snaps of burning pain streaked across Martin's back. Then his buttocks. Then the backs of his thighs. Grunts escaped him with each stroke of Declan's leather belt.

Sean's maniacal laugh erupted to his left.

The strokes began again. The pain sharper this time as previous welts broke open.

It was all too much. In his mind Martin went to a safe place. It usually involved imagining himself on a deserted sun-drenched beach—with a cigarette. This time in his mind's eye, he saw his father.

Chapter Eleven

S hona sat with Davy in the storeroom two doors down the long corridor, her back chocked against a box of who-knows-what. She shook—shaking to her core. Her hands trembled as she hugged herself. She could still feel the pinch of the creep's hand on her breast.

Bastard.

"You okay, Shona?"

"What do *you* think?" she snapped back, and then took a breath. Davy was only being nice. Concerned. Or scared he was next with whatever they were doing to Martin. Thuds echoed down the hall. There had been groans, but they'd stopped now.

Davy swallowed hard, his Adam's apple bobbing crazily.

Silence from the kitchen.

Murmurs from the occupants of the nearby room—women most likely, from the click of high heels as they'd passed the pantry.

It was like the whole house was listening to Martin's punishment.

Footsteps paused outside the door of the room that was now their cell. The door opened and Martin landed on the floor. He was barely conscious as he rolled onto his side and moaned. Shona scooted beside him.

"Martin?" Shona touched his shoulder.

He flinched and gasped.

"Davy, help me," she whispered. "Unpack those blankets over there."

Davy stepped up and ripped the plastic off two of the bundles, and placed the cotton blankets, double folded length ways, on the floor. He came over and took Martin under one arm and Shona took him under the other. Martin groaned awake while they stood him and stepped him to the blankets.

"Lie down here, Martin." Shona helped him lie front down.

The back of his shirt was ripped in places and blood oozed through. Damp, dark patches also spotted his trousers. Shona gasped.

"Get me a new blanket, Davy. Don't open it." She leaned closer to Martin's ear. "I'll have to tend to your wounds, Martin."

"No, don't." Martin lifted his head, started, then rested it down again, the side of his face with the healing yellow bruise uppermost. "You'll not be able to clean it. Just leave it. I'm not bleeding to death, am I?"

"No." Her voice was small. "I'm sorry, Martin." She touched his arm.

He winced, his face crinkled at the brow and his mouth a grimace.

"Why?" Martin breathed deeply. "It's not your fault that creep molested you." His voice muffled into the blankets.

Davy placed the unopened blanket bag next to her. "I found some orange juice. You should drink something, Martin." He placed the small carton of juice beside Martin.

"We have to get out of here." Martin spoke deep and low.

"You're in no state—" Shona began.

"But I will be soon. Then we're going." Martin's arm lay by his thigh, near where she squatted beside him. His fingers pressed together and gave a soft click.

"How?" Davy asked. "Didn't you try that already? Wasn't that how you got your black eye?"

Martin's fingers continued to click. Shona's heartbeat echoed in her chest. The clicking—she'd seen Martin do that before... when his mind was working.

"What's in the boxes in this room?" Martin asked.

Davy rummaged around looking in the boxes, crates, and tubs that filled the room except for the small space they occupied by the door.

"Quietly," Shona whispered.

Martin closed his eyes. Shona brushed his shoulder-length hair away from his face and tucked it behind his ear. His tufty beard was endearing, somehow. He was reasonably handsome. No stunner, but boy did he have brains. She'd never met anyone so smart, nor found brains attractive before.

But *he* was. And he had guts. He'd stopped that creep.

Weeping welled up in her once more and her shoulders shook. She turned her head away. She wouldn't let Martin hear her cry.

"It's okay, Shona. We're getting out of here." He reached his hand up and touched her back, warm and gentle. "Do you feel that breeze coming through the crack at the bottom of the door?"

Shona faced the door. Coolness caressed her cheek. "Aye."

"That's coming from the broken wall of the house. In the room opposite. It's our way out."

Davy scuttled back to them. "I've found torches." He smothered his excitement to a squeaky whisper. "And fresh clothes. We've been in our clothes for over two weeks. And well, Martin's have had it now." He glanced down at Martin's back. The bloodstains had stopped expanding. "Are you sure we can do this?"

"We've got to." Martin breathed a little more evenly, his fingers resumed their quiet, slow clicking.

Davy looked at Shona, his brows crinkled.

"Aye, we must," she spoke to Davy, but her eyes returned to Martin's bruised face. "Declan's got it in for him. He won't be happy until he does some permanent damage." She snapped her head up. "Besides, no one has the right to own another human being. No one!" She clenched her hands into fists. "I'll be no man's slave. And neither will you."

"What about *them*?" With a nod, Davy indicated the room next door but one, where they'd housed the new captives.

"We'll send someone back for them. They'll hinder our escape. We must be silent when we leave." Martin's gruff whisper settled the matter. "The guards do a round near midnight but are pretty slack because, so far, we've behaved ourselves at night."

"But not tonight." Shona leaned down and pressed her lips gently on Martin's cheek. He turned to look at her, his eyes wide and lips parted. She smiled and stood, emotions swirling, and went and chose some clothing for herself and Martin.

Martin regained his strength by the moment. He'd told Davy to keep one torch and look for a knife and duct tape. Davy found them in a box full of stuff that looked like it came from a camping shop. Footsteps passed the door close to midnight. Then all was silent for another hour. Martin sat up and put a shirt on straight over his own bloodied one. Shona handed him a larger size dark coat. She and Davy had already dressed.

"Follow me and do *not* speak," Martin whispered.

He got on his hands and knees and crawled to the door. In the door jamb at floor level was a piece of flat metal. The door hadn't closed properly and therefore not locked. It now opened with ease. Behind Shona, Davy took a breath to speak. She spun and clamped her hand on his mouth. He nodded. She took her hand away.

Shona turned to Martin, a smile tugging her mouth at his brilliance. How had Martin thought to do that on the way back from a thrashing? He must've ripped some of the old metal edging from that monster of a kitchen table that Declan had spread him over for his beating.

Martin checked all was clear, then led them across the hallway and into the opposite room. Lloyd's men had covered the broken wall with tarpaulins in a rough manner. The wind blew cool through the gaps in the tarps. Martin stuck his head through the tarps and checked once more for guards. He brought his head back in, smiling, and took out the pocketknife they'd got from the stores. Shona was thankful their captors hadn't thought that one through when they hastily changed their cells.

After widening the gap, Martin eased himself through, a grimace crossing his face. Shona followed, staying close to the wall as Davy made his way out. Martin pulled the tarp closed behind them and pinched it tightly with some tape from the camping boxes.

Chapter Twelve

The rubble of the mansion's broken wall shifted. A stone pinged lightly on the ground beside Martin as Shona and Davy followed him out. Martin picked up a hefty stone and indicated to Shona and Davy to do the same. They couldn't get out of this without weapons, but whatever happened, they *must* be quiet. He turned and placed his forefinger over his lips, directing his gaze to Davy.

Davy nodded and held up the fist-sized piece of masonry he'd chosen. Martin lifted his chin in acknowledgement. Shona showed her decent-sized chunk of stone.

Martin stepped to the end of the building and poked his head around the corner. Cigarette smoke hit his nostrils and he caught his breath. Then he inhaled deeply, momentarily savouring an old friend. A glance told him two guards were at the back door, their shadows cast long in the light spilling from the door's transom window. Martin pulled back and faced Shona and Davy and held up two fingers, then ushered them back a couple of steps.

"You stay here," Martin whispered. "I'm going to cause a disturbance. When you hear the guards leave, run for the trees on the opposite side of the driveway, then head down the side road. Stay in the cover of the forest 'till I get there. Okay?"

Shona nodded slowly; her brow knotted. Davy took a breath. Martin shook his head and placed his hand over Davy's mouth.

"Just do it!" His voice was a harsh whisper. "Run when you can, okay?"

They both nodded, wide-eyed and hands trembling.

Martin ran along the back of the house, his trousers tugging at his newly formed scabs. He picked up some smaller masonry when he reached the pile he'd made just over a fortnight ago, and ducked under windows even though the lights were out. No sound came from inside the mansion as he skirted its perimeter. Good, all were asleep—maybe.

A breeze stirred the trees at the front of the house. Martin breathed in through his mouth, taking in the night air. He could taste the salt on the light wind. They were nearer to the coast than he had first estimated. He glanced to his right at the grey body of water they would head for. Kirkcaldy and the Firth of Forth was that way. And help. He scuttered along to the far corner. The guard's voices mumbled low through the night air.

Martin threw the smallest of his rocks as far as he could toward the road at the front of the house. He stifled a gasp as his shirt, which had stuck to his back, ripped off more scabs. The stone clattered on the bitumen, then guards stopped talking. They resumed their discussion after a moment's silence. Martin threw another stone, aiming closer to the front fence. No conversation again, then footsteps approached. Martin's heart pounded, and his scalp cooled with his gathering sweat.

He had two chances. The first would be a surprise. The second...well, he'd spent the rest of his time in his safe place, while enduring his beating, recounting his Tae Kwon Do kicks and punches. Muscle memory. The research said replaying a physical routine in your mind helped you perform it in reality. Now he'd know for sure if these theories were true.

The first of Lloyd's men passed the corner of the house. Martin held the heaviest of his rocks high. He used gravity to aid the force of his downward stroke. He struck the guard's temple with maximum power. Skull bone crunched. The man went down with barely a sound. His pal was close behind him. Martin stepped up, taking his stance. His right hand snapped out, using all his strength coming from his shoulder. The rock he held smashed the guard's face as the man's rifle came up. A grunt and a thud.

The guard was down, his rifle sending out a muffled clatter as it hit the front lawn.

Martin blinked. That was too simple. His heart slammed against his rib cage and his mouth dried. He spun to his left. Two heads poked out the side of the back corner of the house. He waved Shona and Davy to him.

Why were they still just standing there! If silence wasn't so important, he'd rip into them!

The guard at his feet groaned. Yep, it had been too easy. He'd have to hit him again.

Don't think, Martin. Just do it!

Gritting his teeth, he tightened his hand around the rock he still held and flicked another punch in the already smashed face. Blood sprayed over his hand and the rock slipped out.

"Oh!" Shona's sharp intake of breath signalled her and Davy's arrival.

"Run!" Martin whispered.

He picked up the rifle, slung it over his shoulder, then followed.

The trees seemed aeons away. His thighs burned and his back stung; muscles recently beaten twinged and complained. The rifle banged against the welts on his right flank.

Davy lagged behind. Martin turned and grabbed him by the arm, pulling him forward while he shushed Davy's grunts. Shona kept up a close pace as they ran over a stubbled field of newly cut hay. The trees were in sight.

They finally ducked into the cool night shade of the copse lining the edge of the road Martin had used on his previous escape attempt.

They hunkered down beside the broadest trunk.

Silence came from the house.

"We made it?" Davy's question was like an announcement over the countryside's public address system.

"Ssh!" Martin echoed with Shona.

Silence still at the house.

"Let's keep moving," Martin ordered in a low voice. "Kirkcaldy's that way."

They walked keeping to the cover of the trees. Houses edged the road here and there.

They knocked on one, but no one answered, despite the lights coming on and footsteps at the door inside.

"People are scared. They can see the gun." Shona tugged at Martin's arm. "Let's just get to Kirkcaldy. The police can help us."

They walked a little further. Torchlight flickered far behind them, back near the mansion-prison they had left. Martin kept them in the cover of the trees for the light of the moon would make them quite visible if they came out and walked the road to Kirkcaldy. He'd not get them caught. *Not going to make that mistake again.*

A vehicle approached; its engine roaring louder as it neared. They sprinted to the thickest part of the tree cover.

"Was that them?" Davy asked.

"Probably," Martin said. "They'll be looking for us in the town as well as around here." He clicked his fingers beside his thigh. "We need to find somewhere to hide till daylight. Then we'll go straight to the police."

"But shouldn't we go to the police now?" Davy's words came out in a rush.

"There's a high probability they'll catch us on the way there," Martin replied.

"Aye, the police station is on the far side of town. We have tae cross right through it to reach it." Shona sat taller as she leaned against the tree beside him. "I ken a place to hide."

"Where?" Martin asked. "Is it close?"

"Where I'm thinkin' of is right by the water. Ravenscraig Castle. We can cut through the golf course to get there."

"But that castle's a ruin." Davy pulled the brand-new jacket tightly around him, the ticket flicked under his chin.

"Exactly." Shona faced Martin; her large brown eyes glinted in the moonlight. "They won't even think to look there. We'll be fine till morning, at least."

Martin slowly nodded. "Aye. Sounds ideal."

After twenty minutes they reached the golf course, and once through it, they kept close to the cover of trees, drystone walls, and houses. They made their way by the outskirts of Kirkcaldy and then kept low to the wall above the beach. Martin glanced back as they crossed the modern equivalent of the castle's drawbridge traversing the deep trench of the moat, a wooden walkway conveniently supplied by Historic Scotland.

Martin turned and scanned as wide as he could see.

No one followed.

Chapter Thirteen

Martin followed Davy and Shona as they walked through the arched gateway of the castle ruins. The cold air from the thick stone walls chilled his face. Once through the tunnel-like entrance, the ruin opened for them to a long and narrow space, the castle complex having been built on a high spine of sandstone jutting out above the beach below. The tide was in, and the waves crashed in a constant rhythm. The cool salty breeze brushed through Martin's hair and he pushed his long fringe out of his eyes and tucked it behind his ear. Night birds called in the wooded parklands beside the castle ruins.

The area in front of him was mostly green grass and low stone walls, the remains of the castle now a *floor-plan* of the fortress. Ahead, and out to sea, the original inhabitants would have seen their enemies approaching. But Martin's enemies would come from the other direction. He turned, in the moonlight a sandstone structure ran along behind them, the remnants of the castle's round towers and main keep. Doors of wrought iron kept tourists out of rooms still intact with a roof. Back toward the sea, rubble and a half-demolished round tower and wall stood closer to the cliff's edge, its sandstone glowing a soft yellow in the moonlight.

"We could shelter over there." Shona pointed to a broken wall at the edge of the sandstone spine, nearest the water, with the beach far below it.

"Aye, but we'd have to jump over the edge if they came." Martin turned to inspect the entrance once more. "We'll have to keep an eye out that way."

"I'll do that," Davy offered. "You need to rest now, Martin."

"Aye, ye look exhausted, Martin." Shona placed her warm hand on his forearm. It was the only part of his body that didn't hurt.

"Take the rifle, Davy." Martin held it out to him. "In case they come."

"No, no, no." Davy waved his hands in front of him, a panicked expression on his face. "I know nothing about guns."

Martin sighed and walked closer to the wall nearest the sea, drawn by the rhythmic crash-and-receding song of the waves below. The moon was behind him, beginning its descent. His limbs dragged, and a heaviness settled in between the flashes of pain. Sitting on the grass, its softness lured him to rest lying on his side. He placed the rifle at his head. Davy's footsteps receded to the stone archway entrance.

"We need food." Shona sat beside him, her body-heat radiating toward him in the cool night.

He shook his head. "We have higher priorities. Like surviving."

"I'll no' go back and be a slave." She echoed her previous words. "I cannae believe I'm speaking like this. A *slave!*' Tears choked in her voice. "That's what that guy, Lloyd, said we'd be. What we *are*." Shona turned her face to him in the moonlight, her brown eyes were like black dots.

Martin took a deep breath in, the skin on his back burned. He didn't answer her. What if Lloyd's men caught them? What if his father couldn't come up with the money? Would he be a slave until he tried to escape again? He didn't know. But one thing was for certain, the world was a different place now.

"I'll no' let them make me into something I'm not." Shona's voice was close to his ear.

Martin blinked as thoughts came spilling back. Things he'd pondered in the dark of the Victorian pantry.

"Even if they catch us, I'll be free," he said.

"Huh? What are you talking about?"

"*Who are you*, Shona?"

"What?" Her tone held a tinge of incredulity.

"You're more than a girl from Wester Hailes," he said. "I know that now."

Shona sat up and blinked but made no comment.

"I labelled you when I first met you. A girl from a rough part of Edinburgh. Just like I'd regard myself as a guy from a nice part of town." He leaned up on his elbow. "A university student studying physics." He shrugged. "I must be smart. A guy from a wealthy family who could have, and do, whatever he wanted." Martin laid back and flinched then sat up again, letting the pain of torn skin pass.

"What're you saying?" Shona tilted her head.

"The world has changed. Lloyd is *so* right. Sadly." He gave a short soft laugh. "Everything I held dear has been taken from me. Uni's over. I don't even know where my father is, let alone if he has any money to pay Lloyd for me." He snorted out a breath. "For all I know, if the current crisis continues, I'll be a slave for the rest of my life if I can't escape that man."

In the half-light, Shona's brow creased.

"I'll be a slave if I can't escape, but I'll be a *free* one." His determination held his voice firm this time.

Shona shook her head slowly. "I really need to understand or I'm gonna think you're going mad."

"I'm not, Shona." Martin reached for her hand. It was calloused from fence building but warm. She gave it, and he held tight to it. "In the core of my being, what is truly me, is more than what I do. Or who my parents are. And so much more than the labels others place on me. Or even the ones I've put on myself willingly. I can be free being *me*, no matter what situation I'm in."

"You *want* to get caught?"

"No! I'll fight tooth and nail for my freedom. But while others think they have power over me, they won't. I refuse to be defined by the roles others assign to me—like *slave*." Voicing his thoughts had a liberating effect. He found his words validated his feelings.

Shona leaned forward; her head shadowed in the waning moonlight. Her lips pressed onto his. Martin hesitated, then returned her kiss. The emotions fighting in his chest were over-ridden by the sense of her—of Shona. And the warmth her lips, her presence, and their relationship gave him. He smoothed down the inner protest and lifted his hand to her cheek. He held her face to his and played his lips over hers. She continued kissing him, her breath warming his face.

She broke away, the moonlight revealing her smile. Then she rubbed her lips together and ran her tongue along them as though she was tasting him.

Man, they didn't have time for any of that, but she was the best thing about this surreal situation he'd found himself in.

She was the noblest cause—a reason to fight.

But the night was slipping away, and they needed to get to help.

"What!" Davy's voice sounded strangled in the pale pre-dawn light. "No.... Martin!"

Chapter Fourteen

D avy stumbled out of the tunnelled archway entrance. Declan pushed him with one hand. The other held a handgun to Davy's head. Davy's wide eyes streamed tears and his lips trembled.

"I'm sorry, Martin." Sobs wrenched through Davy's words.

Martin grabbed the rifle and stood, ignoring burning muscles and searing wounds.

"Dinnae be the stupid eejit *slave* ye are, Moffatt." Hatred wrapped around every word from Declan. Behind him Sean followed, a smug grin filled his face, and his hands jiggled the handgun and walkie-talkie he carried.

"I'm serious. I'll shoot this podge if ye dinnae put the rifle doon!" Declan shook Davy vigorously and pressed the handgun harder into his skull. Davy flinched and a fear-filled gasp escaped his mouth.

Martin lowered the rifle to the ground. His hands shook. Trembling had begun in his arms and was making its way to his core. Shona grabbed his hand, hers shaking too.

"Get them." Declan nodded in their direction.

Sean strode behind them, clipping the walkie-talkie into his belt, and pushed them both to the ground.

"Aw, isn't that sweet. The *slaves* are holding hands." Sean's sarcasm sounded behind them as he forced Shona onto her knees. She grunted.

"Separate them!" Declan yelled then forced Davy to a kneeling position six feet directly in front of them, facing side-on.

Sean ripped Martin's hand from Shona's and pushed him onto his knees. He cocked his handgun at Shona's head and grabbed a handful of Martin's hair. Martin's mouth dried. He glanced sideways to Shona. Her breath came in short gasps, then her lips clamped together, and she breathed loudly through her nose. She returned his stare.

"Now, you lot are causing me a wee bitty too much trouble," Declan growled. "I'm thinkin' the flack I'm going tae get from ma boss is worth puttin' up with, jist tae be rid of yoo trouble-makers. The only one o' ye possibly worth anything is the poncy rich-kid." His glare bore into Martin. "For *Daddy* may just come through with the goods." His fingers flickered around the grip of the handgun he pressed into the back of Davy's head. "So, I've had enough o' this."

Declan's fingers tapped the handgun's stock panel as his features hardened.

The shot echoed off the ruins of Ravenscraig Castle, the bullet's firing cracking the air.

Martin flinched, his hair in Sean's grasp tugging at his scalp.

Shit!

Shona shrieked beside him. Alarmed birdcalls rang from the nearby trees and seagulls on the beach beneath them screeched their startled cries. Davy slumped forward, his face disintegrated by the bullet's exit, and landed front down on the soft green grass.

Numbness hit Martin. The trembling threatened to overtake him. He started breathing again, his heart's thundering continued. He turned to Shona. She was of no value to Declan. Her cheeks streamed with tears. Her face grew paler in the early dawn light.

"You'll get into deep shit with Lloyd over this," Martin spat at Declan.

Declan screwed up his face. "Maybe I will. But I dinnae care." He stepped around Davy's body to stand in front of Shona. "Ma only regret is that I cannae get rid o' you sae easily, *slave*," he said to Martin then pointed the handgun to Shona's head, pressing it in the centre of her brow.

Her forehead crinkled, her mouth trembling as she tried to clamp it shut.

"No, don't!" Martin shouted at Declan and tried to stand. The thundering of his heart now reached his temples.

Sean pulled tighter on the clump of Martin's long hair, burning his scalp at the roots, and held him back in a kneeling position. The cold of the nozzle of Sean's handgun pressed into his neck.

"Keep still." Sean wrenched his head back, eyeballing him. "Enjoy the show."

Declan's fingers flickered around the handgun's grip as he pressed it into Shona's forehead.

Static sounded from the walkie-talkie at Sean's belt.

"Boss wants to know where ya are. Over."

"Shite! Get that," Declan screamed at Sean.

Sean released his tight grasp on Martin's hair and unclipped the walkie-talkie from his belt. "Kirkcaldy. Over."

"'Ave you got 'em?" It was Cockney.

Sean paused. Declan glared at him.

"Aye. Over."

"Bring 'em back. Mr Moffatt's come up with the money. Boss wants you back now. Moffatt won't 'and anything over 'till 'e knows 'is son's alive and well. Over."

Static hissed behind Martin while Declan's brows drew together.

"What do I tell 'em?" Sean asked.

"Don't kill her. My father'll pay for her too." Martin forced all the conviction he could into his voice. "Surely your boss will reward you for a job well done and you'll get a cut."

Declan's mouth was a thin line. He pulled the handgun away from Shona.

"Give me that!" He snatched the walkie-talkie out of Sean's hand.

"Tell Lloyd the slave's negotiatin' for the girl. Over." Declan spoke into the walkie-talkie.

"What? Over."

"Check with Lloyd if Moffatt will pay for the girl too. At his son's request. Over."

Static hissed for a few moments.

Sweat drenched Martin's back, stinging open wounds. Shona's chest heaved rapidly. She fixed her eyes on him, gratitude tinged her frightened expression. A question hung in the air between them.

What if his father didn't have enough?

The static burst through again.

"Moffatt's willin' ta pay. You're to bring 'em 'ere unharmed. Over."

"Aye. Over." Resentment laced Declan's reply, then he threw the walkie-talkie back to Sean.

"Get up," Declan snarled at Martin then directed his venom at Shona. "And you've had a reprieve."

Sean dragged them to their feet and marched them toward the castle's exit.

"What about...Davy?" Martin twisted behind to Davy's slumped body. It was motionless and staining the grass a deep red.

"Leave it!" Declan forced Martin's head around as he dragged Shona along.

"You can't leave him like that!"

"Aye, I can and I am. Shut it."

The van was in the park's grounds, a five-minute walk away. That's why Davy hadn't heard anything. *Poor Davy.* Martin took in a shuddering breath. Shona had nearly ended up the same. He glanced over at her. She was pale and shaking as she stumbled along in Declan's grasp. Dried tears left streak marks on her face. She could still end up dead.

They weren't out of this yet.

Chapter Fifteen

Shona and Martin landed heavily on the floor of the storeroom. The door slammed shut behind them and orders muffled through the door meant a guard was posted outside.

Shona's shoulders shook. She'd been holding it in, but there was no point now. The sharpness of fear gave way to shock and anger at Davy's murder. Her own fate still hung in the balance. Sobs came out, and taking in air was almost impossible.

Martin's arm slipped around her shoulder.

"Breathe." His deep voice, soft in her ear, and the warmth of his arm folding around her were the only soothing things in this confused and scary moment. "Deeply in." Martin demonstrated what he meant. "And out."

Shona took shaky breaths at first but eventually matched his breathing.

"My father will get us out of this." He pressed his lips to her temple.

She continued the rhythmic breathing he'd started and soon was warm and safe tucked under his arm.

"How's this going to work?" she asked.

"My father will get the money and—"

"No, I mean *us*."

Martin looked at her, an eyebrow cocked. "Let's just get out of this."

Heavy footsteps tramped up and down the corridor. To their left, where Lloyd's library was, the men were having a conflab. The door to the library opened and their voices got louder as the men approached the door of their storeroom-cell.

"Out!" Declan pointed a handgun at them while Lloyd walked past the now open door.

Sean stopped Shona just outside the door and tied her hands with plastic pull-ties. He did the same to Martin. Then he shoved them forward and they followed Declan's back down the corridor to a waiting van. Lloyd was in the front seat and all the men had guns. They pushed Shona into the back and jolted her onto the floor of the van next to Martin.

What if they shot Martin's father? Then her, and Martin? Lloyd would still get the money.

Shona turned to Martin.

"No talking!" Declan kicked Martin in the back. Martin recoiled, and his brow creased in pain.

The sky passed by Shona's view out the side window of the van. Dark clouds patched it here and there. The shadow of trees flickered for a while then moved away. Then the road sound changed and the view at the sides became clear, like a Perspex wall. Behind this, poles and thick ropy wire rose in long modern lines. Seagulls hovered next to the road. They were on the new bridge, the Queensferry Crossing. Shona nudged Martin. He turned his gaze from the window and nodded only slightly. He'd probably guessed it too. They were on their way into Edinburgh, no doubt.

Once over the new bridge, they turned off sharply. Shona's mouth dried, now unsure of their destination. She touched Martin with her toe and raised her eyebrows in question. He shrugged almost imperceptibly. The men in the van had remained silent the whole journey.

The road narrowed and now old stone buildings encroached her view, and the van's motion pushed Shona about on the floor. She rolled into Martin when the van made a sharp left.

"There he is," Lloyd said from the front seat. "Stop here. He's got some muscle with him."

The van's brakes squeaked, and they pulled up.

"Stay here," Lloyd ordered. "This man is a gentleman. I'll deal with him."

Martin made to move but Declan kicked him. Martin winced and stayed low.

"But my father—"

Declan leaned down and spoke firmly into Martin's face. "Shut it."

Lloyd's footsteps echoed away from the van. Voices reached them. Martin stiffened beside her. Had he heard his father? The van door slid open and banged.

"Up." Declan nudged Martin.

Martin stood but refused to move. "And Shona," he said, looking toward the front of the van. His chest heaved and he blinked rapidly. He turned back to Declan. "I'm not moving without her."

"Martin?" A man's voice with a well-spoken Scottish accent called from a few meters away.

"Shona has to come," Martin said. "You're paying for her too, right?"

"Aye. Lloyd, the lass too." The man's voice held authority. "That's the deal and the money's all there."

Declan bent down and pulled Shona out. She stood; the glare of the grey day surprising. They were on the old stone Queensferry wharf right on the river Forth. To her right were the masts of sailboats, the boats themselves lower than the wharf due to the low tide. Ahead, on the narrow stone walkway, stood Lloyd. Beside him, a tall man with a strong likeness to Martin and greying hair, neatly styled, wore a sports jacket and a serious expression. The man held a bag which bulged and dragged on his arm. A white luxury class SUV, with a man in the driver's seat, parked side-on behind him.

"Walk," Declan ordered with a shove.

Shona and Martin reached Martin's father and Lloyd.

"Get to the car, son." Martin's father spoke low and firm.

Martin nodded and nudged her to keep going toward the vehicle. The walk to the open door of the SUV took forever.

"There. Deal done," Martin's father said behind them.

Gunshots clapped from Lloyd's men. A bullet whizzed past Shona's ear. Martin dragged her the last few paces and shouldered her into the open car door. A thud hit her back. Martin pushed her low into the seat and leaned on top of her. Martin's father ran behind.

Click-clack came from the front seat of the vehicle and a gun fired through the open passenger window. Shona's ears rang. The engine revved as Martin's father clambered into the seat beside them.

"Get going!" Martin's father screamed at the driver.

That *click-clack* sounded again, but right beside Shona. Martin's father fired as they screeched past the van.

More ringing in her ears.

Bullets shattered windows and Lloyd's men returned the gunfire. Small pieces of broken glass fell around her, covering the carpeted floor of the vehicle. Glass fragments showered down from Martin who leaned over her.

Bullets pinged on metal. A grunt came through the open front passenger window. They must have passed close to Lloyd's van.

Their vehicle skidded up the stone wharf to the narrow main street of Queensferry, gunfire ringing around them all the way.

Shona's back roared at her. A searing pain to her left side replaced the initial numbness after the thud to her back.

Martin's father dropped the rifle in the front seat.

"Get us out of here, Ali," Mr Moffatt yelled at the driver.

"Martin?" Shona grabbed at Martin's arm, her hands, like his, still in their plastic bonds.

Martin turned and looked down at her. "Dad! We need to get to a hospital. Shona's been shot."

Chapter Sixteen

The ride to Edinburgh Royal Infirmary was interminable. Martin pressed Shona's side once the blood seeped through her clothing. Lloyd's van hadn't followed. Martin breathed out a long sigh. They pulled up in front of the Emergency Department. His father ran in and came out with a patient trolley and a nurse.

"Oh, I thought so," the nurse said to Martin. "You're Caitlin's cousin, Martin. And you must be her Uncle Kieran," she spoke to his father. "I recognised you from her photos."

"Aye, we are, but we have a young woman with a gunshot wound." His father helped Shona onto the gurney.

They rushed inside and raced through the corridor to the main treatment area where people sat on or around patient trolleys. IV poles stuck out in their pathway and staff sped past them. Monitors beeped, and people shouted orders. Babies cried, and moans of pain filtered from behind curtains.

"A resus bay has just become free. Go to Bay Seven!" The younger nurse then called to an older woman. "Milla, come."

Milla pulled the curtains to Bay Seven behind her. "Jan"—she waved the younger nurse closer then spoke low— "Others have been waiting longer."

"Aye, I know but this girl had a gunshot wound. It's Caitlin's Uncle Kieran." She pointed to Martin's father. "And that's Martin," she said, indicating him.

"Oh, hi," Milla said, her shoulders relaxing.

Jan and Milla worked on Shona. A Dr Kumran came into the cubicle and gave some orders to them.

"The bullet has passed through," Dr Kumran told Martin's father. "So we'll clean her up and she should be fine with some antibiotics to prevent infection,"

"How's Caitlin? She's not turned up for work yet." Jan's big eyes peered into Martin's face. "She was due back last week. I went around to her flat, but I couldn't get an answer."

"And we can't get her on her mobile, now that they're working again, sort of," Milla said, opening a dressing pack out onto a treatment trolley.

Martin turned to his father whose expression was grave, and he chewed his lip.

"Dad?" Martin's neck cooled. "Have you found her yet?"

"What do you mean 'found her'?" Jan's gaze flicked from Martin to his father.

A chill ran down Martin's spine.

His father took a deep breath. "Caitlin went missing when our home was ransacked nearly a month ago." He shook his head. "We haven't heard from her since."

"Have you looked?" Jan sounded accusing.

"Excuse me." Martin's father stood straighter and pierced the younger nurse with his gaze. "I have tried to get the police to look for her but gave up because they're so busy. I've hired a PI, not that it's really any business of yours."

Jan looked at the floor. "I'm sorry. I just..." She walked out of the cubicle.

"Jan?" Milla called after her, and then returned to dressing Shona's side.

Martin sat by Shona and held her hand while Milla cleaned the bullet wounds, front and back, and stuck bandages on them.

"Who's Caitlin?" Shona looked up at Martin.

"She's my first cousin and..." Martin shrugged. "We don't know where she is or if she's even alive." His throat closed over and he leaned forward, resting his head on Shona's shoulder. It was comfortable, and he could breathe there. She didn't flinch, and her hand came up and touched his hair, and stayed.

"Thank you, Mr Moffatt," Shona said over Martin's head.

"You're welcome, Shona."

"How'd you get the money?" Martin flicked his head up from Shona's shoulder. "I thought you said we'd lost everything."

"Remember what I taught you, son? Those that have money know how to borrow it, make it, and keep it." His father chuckled. "I must admit, with this crash it wasn't easy. I've had to call in many favours."

The curtain to Resus Bay Seven skidded open on its rail then a policeman stepped in behind Jan.

"I hear you have a gunshot wound to be reported," he said.

"Aye, and a murder," Martin said. "And a missing person."

"And kidnap." Martin's father had spoken at the same time. "A murder? What are you talking about, son?"

"In the grounds of Ravenscraig Castle ruins you'll find a body of a young man," Martin spoke directly to the policeman. "He's Davy McMichael." Martin's words caught in his throat.

His father then gave the policeman the details of Caitlin's unaccounted-for-absence, Martin's kidnapping, and the situation at Queensferry.

"Och, well." The officer shook his head. "I'll make my reports and you come to the station and give your statements but I cannae promise much action at present. We are inundated with work."

"I can well imagine," Martin's father commented.

"I dinnae think ye can, actually." The policeman's shoulders lifted in a sigh. "Just between you, me, and the gatepost"—the officer leaned close to Martin's father— "the cache of illegal weapons, which have been stored at police headquarters since the last amnesty, has been stolen. There are more guns, knives, automatic machine guns and God-knows-what out there now than there ever has been." He tilted his head. "If I were you, and had the means, I'd hide away until all this shite settled down." He nodded and left the cubicle.

Martin blinked. It couldn't get worse, could it?

His father spun back to them. "Right, are we done, Milla?"

Milla nodded. "Just need that script for antibiotics filled."

"Aye. Thank you," he said and took the script from Milla.

Jan opened the curtains for them.

"You okay?" Martin helped Shona sit up.

"Aye." She looked at him and then at his father.

"This is what we'll do." His father leaned in close to them. "We're getting your mother, sisters and anybody else." He paused and looked at Shona. "Shona, we'll stop by your home on the way. You live in Edinburgh, don't you?"

Shona nodded, her brow furrowed, either in pain or in concern over what his father was saying.

"We are going." Martin's father looked him in the eye. "We'll find a safe place to ride out this mess."

"And Caitlin?" Martin asked. "We can't go without Caitlin."

"We'll still search for her, son."

"But—" Shona stiffened under Martin's arm.

"What?" Martin turned to her.

Shona took a breath. "Should we no' stay and call the Government to action?'

"No, Shona." Martin's father shook his head. "Let's be safe until the trouble settles down. It's spiralling out of control out there, and we need something to hold onto while it does. We've got to survive this, so we can fight another day. That's what's called for at present. We can bother the Government from a secure hiding place."

Martin straightened and held tight to Shona. She stood, and he tucked her by his side, following his father past beeping IV pumps and monitors. Once outside, the afternoon sun warmed Martin in the calm carpark.

He lifted his face to sunshine and breathed in deep. The world was changing.

No. He shook his head.

It *had* changed, and would never be the same relatively secure world in which he'd grown up.

He glanced down at Shona. They'd be together, and safe with his family. He'd make sure of it.

Then he'd find a way to make it all right again.

In time.

Afterword

Meet Martin again in the next three novels in the *Community Chronicles Series*.

Caitlin and Scott feature in *Stolen Time: Community Chronicles Book 2*. Martin is responsible for developing the time machine which features in these novels.

STOLEN TIME:

A YOUNG WOMAN'S DESTINY

AN ILLEGAL TIME TRAVELLER

AND A BOND THAT WILL SHAPE THE FUTURE

"Lees' intense and powerful plotline presents a pulse pounding image of a world suddenly turned upside down...a compelling and provocative portrait of a pair of destined lovers determined to survive." J B Richards. IHIBRP 5 Star Review

About the Author

DESTINY RELATIONSHIP COURAGE

Retired nurse Jenn has travelled extensively and lived on three continents. Although Australia is the land of her birth, Scotland has always called her back. This country remains her source of inspiration, where she now lives with her husband, and close family nearby.

Jenn loves walking through a forest and climbing a mountain to experience the view. Or exploring a castle ruin and soaking in the history. Her only disappointment in life is that time travel is not possible... apparently.

Award-winning fantasy author Jenn Lees' latest release, *Of High Kings and Mages: Arlan's Pledge Book Three,* reached the Semi-Finalist stage in the OZMA Book Awards for Fantasy Fiction 2024 CIBAs (Chanticleer International Book Awards).

Of Warriors and Sages: Arlan's Pledge Book Two reached Semi-Finalist in the OZMA Book Awards for Fantasy Fiction 2023 (as the manuscript *The Quest*). Longlisted in the Realm Awards 2025 Fantasy Section. As the manuscript *The Quest* reached the Top 10 in Ink & Insights 2021.

Jenn Lees' Best Selling novel, *Of Myths And Portals: Arlan's Pledge Book One* achieved First Place Award (Gold) in The BookFest Fall 2024 Fiction-Romance-Fantasy, Second Place Award (Silver) in The BookFest fall 2024 Fiction-Fantasy-Magic, Myths and Legends, and Fiction-Christian-Fantasy

The Crossing: Arlan's Pledge Book 1 (re-released as *Of Myths and Portals*) achieved the finals in the OZMA Book Awards for Fantasy Fiction (previous draft manuscript) CIBA 2021. *Restoring Time* (Book 4 of the *Community Chronicles Series*) reached the finals in the CYGNUS Awards for Science Fiction 2021 CIBA.

An Ink & Insights Competition judge says of *Arlan's Pledge*:

'Beautifully crafted, full of rich setting descriptions, tension that caught my attention and kept it, and characters that leapt off the page. This author is a skilled storyteller.' (Melody Quinn. Ink & Insights 2021 Competition Master Category Judge)

Find out more about Jenn Lees and her novels.

Sign up for the newsletter and receive *Running with the Stags,* a free novella in the *Arlan's Pledge Series.*

www.jennleeswriter.com

Want more of Jenn Lees?   Support Jenn Lees Fantasy Author on Patreon.

https://www.patreon.com/c/jennleesfantasyauthor/members

Also By JENN LEES

THE COMMUNITY CHRONICLES SERIES
Stolen Time: Community Chronicles Book 2
Saving Time: Community Chronicles Book 3
Restoring Time: Community Chronicles Book 4
ARLAN'S PLEDGE SERIES
OF MYTHS AND PORTALS: ARLAN'S PLEDGE BOOK ONE
Destiny must claim them
(Previously published as *The Crossing: Arlan's Pledge Book One*)
OF WARRIORS AND SAGES: ARLAN'S PLEDGE BOOK TWO.
The heart-quest must win
OF HIGH KINGS AND MAGES: ARLAN'S PLEDGE BOOK THREE
A king must die
MURTAIREAN: AN ASSASSIN'S TALE
A novel in the Dál Cruinne Series

All Jenn's novels are also available in eBook and audiobook